Kill City

BALOGUN OJETADE

Copyright © 2019 Balogun Ojetade

All rights reserved.

ISBN-13: 9781686593369

DEDICATION

I dedicate this book to all the serious practitioners and teachers of the martial arts from—and those with roots in--Africa. Keep the culture, principles and techniques alive. For us; by us. Ase O

ACKNOWLEDGMENTS

I would like to thank my students/family of the Afrikan Martial Arts Institute—Akinbobola Kayode Donaldson, Amosun Oyabode (Flux) Singleton, Sangobunmi Gray and Lunar Butterfly (Sangobunmi)—that helped me to create this dope cover! I love y'all and may we continue to do big things together.

I would also like to thank my wife, Iyalogun Ojetade, for her undying support and encouragement. We've loved each other for decades and it just keeps getting better. May we forever grow in love, health, success and prosperity together.

CHAPTER ONE

The killer knew his quarry well. They were all the same—in Thailand, Japan, Kenya, France, America. The master-soon-to-be victim would pad quietly into his training hall hours ahead of everyone else. He trained fighters, but a sound business was a diversified business, and he had branched out into general fitness and health—a big jump for the soon-to-be-victim's bottom line.

For the master, even after fifteen years in America—womanizing, drinking Red Bull and orange vodka in the French Quarter and eating beignets and drinking chicory coffee every day at Café du Monde—he was, despite all his success and debauchery, still a martial artist at heart. Which was why, increasingly, he found himself before dawn, alone in the kwoon—*training hall*—pushing himself further and further, in fierce pursuit of the moment when he and his art became inseparable.

His name was Gunter Wulff, and he had been training in Wing Chun for over forty years. Even though he was in his late-fifties, he was athletically built and very well-toned. Wulff was a professional of the old school. In his time in Atlanta he had led and harassed legions of aspiring black sashes into his demanding vision of the martial arts.

His forearms and fingers were thick and strong from countless hours on the Mook Jong—*wooden dummy*. His feet were tough and dry from hours of work on the hardwood floor of the training hall.

Wulff had come in off the street and changed into his yellow school t-shirt—with *Wulff's Wing Chun* written in red across the back and the school's logo on the chest—black cotton pants and black "kung-fu" shoes.

And then his attacker made his move.

***

The medical examiner's report suggested that Master Wulff was not dead for more than an hour before the building's manager found him at eight-thirty in the morning.

The ritual of the challenge was almost certainly performed. The attacker enjoyed his symbols. The ritual was important. He was most probably dressed in street clothes—it's a bit hard making your getaway dressed in a Tae Kwon Do dobok or Japanese hakama in Atlanta—but he most certainly would have followed all the martial arts etiquette: the bows or salutes, the ritual introductions and presentation of training pedigree, the request for a "comparison."

Detectives figured that the fight would have been fast. Fighters at Wulff's level of proficiency or greater did not waste time. The more time you spent, the more fatigued you got and the more opportunities for error.

Wulff's forearms and shins were bruised from parrying attacks. He had friction marks on his shoulder from rolling on the hard floor. And he had a bruise on the top of his hand between the thumb and index finger, indicating he must have tried a choke at one point—he had tried to slide in the choke and the opponent defended by lowering his chin, using the bone to protect his throat.

The police dusted the floor of the kwoon to get a sense of how things went. The two fighters had fought all over the training hall, ultimately ending up near the weapons rack.

Tiny wood fragments were found along the ridge of the palm—apparently, he had broken one of the six-foot long staffs with a chop. The attacker, wielding what he thought was a potent weapon, must have been momentarily stunned when the power of Wulff's attack snapped the staff in two.

But the recovery was equally sudden. The staff became a spike.

The first strike must have been almost instinctual—a straight thrust, hard and quick, into the midsection. The pain must have been intense for Wulff, but there was no blood—puncture wounds don't bleed except internally.

Did the jagged end of the staff stay buried in Wulff's guts, or did the attacker yank it out right away? It was hard for detectives to tell. Eventually, the loss of blood slowed the Wing Chun master down. And then the attacker finished it.

He plunged that jagged piece of staff into Wulff, perforating his abdomen repeatedly.

Did the attacker enjoy Wulff's gasps each time he drove the weapon home? Did he revel in the growing sense of domination? Did he smile even as Wulff's lips twisted in agony?

The detectives were not sure.

Wulff lay there, one hand outstretched—he had tried to reach the phone on the wall, but died before he got to it.

The killer had paused long enough to leave a clue; and a warning. Scribbled on the wall in Wulff's blood was simply "*1488.*"

CHAPTER TWO

The silence in the old factory was suffocating. The rays of the sun crept in through the high windows, shining a spotlight on the bits of dust dancing about the capacious room.

A short, stout middle-aged man, with mahogany skin strode onto the floor. He was wearing a navy blue bowling shirt and baggy blue jeans. On his head he wore a flat cap that matched his shirt. The brim of the cap was tilted over one eyebrow. His feet, covered in black leather hi-top *Converse All-Star* sneakers, moved cat-like across the concrete floor.

Divine Mathematics' swagger was evident. It was not just the way he was dressed. But in even the smallest action, he was precise, purposeful. He gazed at the score of students standing before him, his round head swiveling slowly up and down the line.

Other than his head, nothing moved, but his students could almost feel the energy pulsing off of him and washing over them.

The students stood eyeing their teacher warily. Faint

sighs could be heard. The students knew they were in for a rough workout. Something about the upturn of the corners of Divine Mathematics' lips said so.

You didn't go to *Black Fists and Afros* without being serious about training and having a love for Black people. The school wasn't easy to find; it was hidden in the SWATS—*Southwest Atlanta*—off Cascade Road, sitting among other warehouses behind *Home Depot*. Divine Mathematics had been teaching in the same location for ten years and everyone in the area respected, or feared, him, but he did not have social media and did not allow his students to create an Instagram, Facebook or Twitter account for the school. He did allow them to post pictures and short videos on their own accounts, so his notoriety began to spread beyond Atlanta.

The neighborhood where the school was located, though inhabited by affluent and middle-class Black families, was bustling and loud. Fast food and fancy restaurants, smoothie bars, coffee houses and car washes, grocery store chains, hardware stores and high-end furniture stores all along Cascade kept an eclectic crowd coming to the area.

Once you got inside *Black Fists and Afros,* however, the rest of the world disappeared. The school—really an old warehouse that Wise Mathematics had converted, smoothing the worn floor and laying down red puzzle mats the entire length then adding heavy bags and battle ropes—was a cavernous space. The walls were painted off-white and on the back wall, painted in black, was "*52 Blocks*Ijakadi*Weapons.*" To one side there was a small office area with a battered green metal desk and two doors leading to the changing rooms. And just outside the office was an oak rack holding scores of metal, but blunt training knives, rubber practice guns, nightsticks, and baseball bats.

Once the lesson started, none of the students spent much time worrying about how tough things were.

"Greetings, family!" Divine Mathematics began. "Today, we're gonna work the first seven foundational techniques of the Fifty-Two—*Skull and Bones, Closed Door, Triangle Trade, Uptown, Read the Book, Cover the Bullet,* and *Open Door*; so let's get to it."

The teacher snapped to attention. "Ago!"

The students followed suit, snapping to attention in unison as they shouted, "Ame," in response.

"Dobale!" Divine Mathematics commanded.

The students and the teacher knelt on their right knees as they raised their left hand to the height of their brow, palm outward, and placed their right fist next to their right knee. They all shouted, "Ogun!"

"Dide," Divine Mathematics said, ordering the students to stand.

And then the training began. Students partnered up and began throwing jabs, crosses, hooks and overhand punches at each other, which were easily deflected by the simple and effective 52 Blocks defenses—various blocks and parries with mainly precise elbow strikes and a few with the palms.

After about an hour of intense training, most of the students were slowing down, shaking their arms and hands in an effort to bring life back to their numb and swollen forearms and to alleviate the pain in the small bones of their hands.

Divine Mathematics let the students take a brief water break then ordered them back onto the mats, where they added ankle picks, single-leg takedowns, sweeps and other quick and deceptive attacks against the legs to off-balance an opponent or make him fall. After an hour of grappling training, Divine Mathematics let the students sit down on the mats and sip water as he moved into what he called the "Building Session."

"Today, we are gonna build with a student that has been with me since I first moved here from Bed-Stuy," Divine Mathematics began. "I always say that this student is part teacher, part preacher and all fighter. She's a chef and does the popular *Urban Vegan* show on Instatube, or Snapgram or whatever y'all call it."

The students laughed.

"Whatever," Divine Mathematics sighed with a wave of his hand. "Y'all give it up for Janiah Mack!"

A young woman in the front of the group of students leapt to her feet and snapped to attention. She was tall and athletically built with smiling eyes that made her pretty face look even more radiant. She had a smooth, medium brown complexion and long, braided black hair, wrapped up in a bun. Most people told her that she looked like a young Regina Hall. She took that as a compliment. Regina Hall was beautiful and a highly talented actor.

Janiah grabbed a metal folding chair and placed its front legs at the edge of the mat next to her teacher then she sat down.

"At Black Fists and Afros, we study the African martial arts," Janiah began. "Fifty-Two Blocks, which is credited to the New York prison system is really African martial arts. Whether it was just in the DNA of the brothers and sisters in the New York jails prisons and streets, or if it was passed down from enslaved Africans is up for debate, but one thing is for sure: it comes from us."

The students clapped.

"We also study Ijakadi," Janiah went on. "Ijakadi is a Yoruba word that means 'combat'. When you go anywhere in West Africa, if you ask for 'martial arts', they will send you to a Tae Kwon Do, Karate or Judo school. You have to ask for 'wrestling' to find African Martial Arts. 'Wrestling', to an African, means 'to put someone on their back, belly, or side... by *any* means'. If you shoot him in the gut and he falls, he was 'wrestled'; if you knock him out with an elbow strike to the temple, he was 'wrestled' by African standards."

"So if they're both African, what's the difference between Fifty-Two and Ijakadi?" a student asked.

"Fifty-Two Blocks is all about the defense," Janiah replied. "To set up your opponent and obliterate him with strikes while keeping him from hitting you. It's about the hand game. Ijakadi is about putting your opponent on his back, belly or side by any means, so Ijakadi incorporates it all—strikes, blocks, knees, kicks, throws, sweeps, reaps, ground fighting and weapons, but it's bread and butter is grappling—throws, clinches, takedowns, sweeps, reaps, chokes. Here, we use Fifty-Two's supreme defensive and striking and Ijakadi's supreme grappling and weapons to create a system that is hard to beat and able to handle anything out on these streets—"

Janiah was going to say something else when movement on the edge of the mat caught her eye.

Visitors filed in swiftly, bending slightly at the waist while hooking their thumbs in their waistbands and making inverted pyramids with their index fingers above their groins in a strange karate-like bow. There were three of them in street clothes and the fourth was dressed in a *black uniform with a red trim down the top's* collar, black panels with a red trim extending from the top's hem and, instead of a belt, a thick black band with a red trim around the waist. He wore a red silk scarf, tucked into the top of his uniform and covering his neck and chest. The uniform was reminiscent of a Korean General's ancient war uniform. The man had obviously come to make a statement.

The visitors sat quietly in the back of the room with their backs against the wall, watching the class with hard-eyed stares and serious expressions.

Divine Mathematics called the class to "Circle up." The students leapt to their feet then quickly formed a circle. They snapped to attention.

The teacher stepped into the circle and looked around at each student. He was avoiding looking at the gang of four in the back of the room, but it was apparent from his body language that he was annoyed.

You don't come to *Black Fists and Afros*, especially dressed in a martial arts uniform, unless you've been invited. If you show up uninvited and suited up at *Black Fists and Afros*, it means one of two things: either you think you live in a Kung-Fu movie and are in danger of being beaten up, or you are purposefully being insulting and want to challenge Divine Mathematics to a match and are in danger of being beaten up.

"Lagbara!" Divine Mathematics ordered. The students relaxed but remained standing with their feet at shoulder-width. Divine Mathematics stepped into the middle of the circle then turned to one of his senior pupils, Yosef, who stood next to Janiah.

"I see we have visitors," the teacher said. "Go invite the one in the monkey-suit to speak with me."

Divine Mathematics and Yosef saluted each other by kneeling, sitting back on their heels and raising their left hands while placing their right fists next to their knees. They rose then Yosef scurried to the back of the room to deliver the invitation. The man in the uniform nodded, exchanged handshakes with his companions, and stepped into the center of the circle of *Black Fists and Afros'* students on the mat. He bowed then stepped wide, bending his knees and bringing his hands out before him, palms down and chest high. The man shouted, "Eeyaaa.

The *Black Fists and Afros* students rolled their eyes.

Divine Mathematics nodded slightly and the uniformed man moved forward.

"Sorry that I wasn't able to welcome you properly to my *school*," Divine Mathematics said, *a broad smile spreading across his face.* "I'm also sorry that I don't know who you are or what you want, since we haven't been properly introduced."

"My name's Alfredo Mejia, Teacher," the man said, bowing deeply. Joo Im Kwahn Jahng Nim, or Head Master of Kuk Sool Won Buckhead."

"So, Mr. Mejia, I assume there's a reason for you coming here," Divine Mathematics said. "Our school is off the beaten path, so only a man in need of something would make the effort to find us."

"I don't *need* anything from anybody, bro'," Mejia said coldly. "I *want* a match." he said. "I'm challenging you."

Divine Mathematics looked back and forth among his

students, weighing each one for potential, for flaws.

"Janiah Mack," he called.

"Yes, sir," Janiah said, snapping to attention.

"This is Ms. Mack," Divine Mathematics told Mejia. "I'm sure you'll get what you came here from her."

Mejia scowled. "I come to challenge you and you have a *female* represent you? What kind of martial artist… hell what kind of man are you? You must be joking, but I'm not fucking around."

"I'm that type of man that trains all my students, men and women, to handle whatever comes their way, Mr. Mejia," Divine Mathematics said. "Even dudes with big egos in clown-ass karate suits. Sorry, but we can't teach you any lessons here. You're clearly not ready to get this work."

With that, Divine Mathematics stepped out of the circle, took a seat and started drinking a bottle of alkaline water.

"Wait a minute—" Mejia stormed past the students toward Divine Mathematics.

As Mejia came at him, Divine Mathematics leapt from his chair and exploded forward. He slammed an elbow strike into Mejia's jaw, stunning him and sending him staggering sideways. Then Divine Mathematics was behind him, a sinewy arm wrapped around Mejia's neck and grasping the bicep of his other arm, which Divine Mathematics pressed against the side of his own head.

The choke was precisely executed. After a few seconds, Mejia fell to the floor out cold.

Divine Mathematics beckoned to Mejia's comrades.

"Get him out of here and don't come back," he said. "Oh, and clean the piss out of his pants with white vinegar."

The uninvited visitors dragged Mejia off the practice floor and carried him away.

"Arrogant fool," Divine Mathematics said, shaking his head.

He sauntered away to his office and the class ended.

CHAPTER THREE

Janiah lived in the West End because the rent was cheaper and *Black Fists and Afros* was only a few miles away, but she shot the *Urban Vegan* show at *Elmwood Studios* in Fayetteville, Georgia, far south of her home.

Elmwood Studios was more expensive than many videographers that lived much closer, but Elmwood was Black-owned and were the best videographers and filmmakers in the South. Her show had won awards for being the highest quality on the internet and that high quality had helped her gain a steady, high-paying clientele that wanted great vegan soul food, including two colleges and nearly every major film shot in Atlanta.

She walked into the teaching kitchen at Spelman College's Wellness Center, where she prepared the meals for events at the school she was paid to cater.

Her mailbox, one in a series of slots labeled with neatly typed paper slips (easily replaced), was filled with the usual junk. There was an announcement about an upcoming faculty meeting—even though she was not faculty, so she wasn't eligible to attend—a brochure encouraging her to join the Master's Program at Spelman, and a message that she was wanted in the office of the Vice President of Business and Financial Affairs.

Janiah headed across campus until she reached Rockefeller Hall. The building's brick building was old and the halls smelt of furniture polish and plaster with a whiff of old paper.

Robert Flanigan, the VP of Business and Financial Affairs was a husky man with smooth, shiny honey-brown skin. He had balding gray hair, which he patted absently in moments of thought and a thin mustache. He was articulate, wily, and immensely pleased with himself.

He didn't get up from behind the desk when Janiah entered his office; he just swiveled around to see her better. "Hey, Ms. Mack," he said. "What have you been up to?" The Vice President was chewing gum furiously and bending a paperclip back and forth.

And he had a plan, which was how, Janiah ended up waiting to meet Spelman's president the next day.

***

President Joseph Nix was an old-style autocrat and had developed serious hang-ups for being criticized as a male president of a women's college, even though Albert E. Manley and Donald M. Stewart had both preceded him by many decades. He was notorious for firing people on the spot, for denying tenure recommendations, and generally outraging the rank and file. He did have a few good points: sometimes he fired people who deserved it and, most important for the college, he was a relentless brown-noser who had managed to raise millions for the institution.

Occasionally, you caught glimpses of him churning across campus with any number of flunkies in his wake, but most contact with him took the form of various memos that ended up in everyone's mailboxes. The president thought of himself as something of an intellectual. He had graduated with a B.A. and a Master's of Educational Administration from Howard University and a PhD in Educational Administration from Emory, so maybe at one time this delusion actually held some water. He was on the far side of sixty now, however, and although he could be eloquent and charming, mostly Nix came across as a boojie old snob.

Flanigan had told Janiah to "dress nicely" for the meeting, which meant that she had to wear the one good business suit she owned—a navy blue skirt with matching suit jacket and a white blouse. The Vice President had been generous with his unsolicited, unwanted gratuitous advice about what to wear and what to say at the meeting and had escorted her to the door of the presidential suite, wished her luck, then hightailed it out of there before Janiah did something that got them both fired.

She sat in the muted air of the president's reception room while prim and efficient secretaries bustled to and fro. Phones chirped discretely. The furniture was made of cherry oak and oxblood leather and everything was polished and dust free.

The door to the president's office finally opened. Polite laughter and the sound of gruff instructions spilled out into the hush and then a cluster of men in suits tumbled out.

Janiah was up. Her basic plan for the interview was to say as little as possible, make the president feel she was competent, and escape with her contract in tact.

President Nix beckoned from behind a desk the size of a pool table, inviting her in, and actually got up to shake her hand.

"Ms. Mack. Good. How are you?" He had what sounded like a Baltimore accent with a little posh British mixed in. He let the words drawl out, as if he enjoyed the way they felt as they came out of his mouth. "Vice President Flanigan tells me that you are as accomplished a martial artist as you are a master chef. Sit down."

Janiah shook President Nix's hand. "Yes, I am a martial artist," she said. "I'm not nearly as good at martial arts as I am at cooking, though." She sat down.

Nix picked up some papers and gave them a quick glance. "A Grand Diplôme from Le Cordon Bleu in Paris," he said with a nod."You beat Bobby Flay cooking on his show, you've written a book of vegan soul food recipes."

He looked up as if he was thinking. "You've been catering Spelman's special events for how long?"

He knew the answer as well as Janiah did. It was right there in front of him. "Three years, sir."

"Three years." He said with a smirk. "Giving us healthy, delicious business lunches and convention meals and impressing investors."

"Yes."

He got a bit more animated then, putting both hands flat on the desk and staring at Janiah intently. "So," he said finally. "I assume Flanigan has described the nature of the assignment?"

"You need someone with expertise in the martial arts to develop some descriptive material for an exhibit being run by a potential donor," Janiah said. "That's fine, sir."

"You understand that remuneration will be coming from the client and not the university?"

Janiah nodded.

"Fine," he said. "My secretary will provide you with the name of the potential donor. Have a good day."

And just like that, it was over. The president leaned back in his seat and whirled away to gaze out the window. Like posing for a portrait: *Brooding Intellectual Surveys His Domain*. The afternoon sun lit up his craggy face and his expensive shark skin suit.

The name that Janiah got from the president's secretary was Nemesio Pena. The martial arts circle in Atlanta was not that large, so she had heard of him. Nemesio Pena had been an early promoter on the Southern grappling tournament scene. He saw the business potential in grappling arts of Jujutsu, Greco Roman and Freestyle Wrestling, Sambo and Judo outside of Mixed Martial Arts and over twenty or so years he had gradually gotten his fingers into every piece of the martial arts pie that he could. He was doing pretty well now, but Janiah was surprised that President Nix was rubbing elbows with him, given Pena's semi-sleazy reputation.

Then again, as the Yoruba say, *"If you have wealth, every dog and goat will claim to be related to you,"* she thought.

Pena had gone upscale, with an office in Buckhead at his Martial Masters museum. Janiah strode through the glass doors off the street and entered the lobby, which featured an eight-foot waterfall splashing down a black rock face. The water-works split the lobby into two parts—one devoted to the museum and the other to offices. Janiah wandered over to the right, to the office suites. The area was sedate, with muted tans and greens, bleached wood panels lining the walls, and paintings of Shaolin monks practicing Kung Fu, sword-wielding samurai and ancient Greek wrestlers. The receptionist was blonde, with ruddy skin, like she had spent too much time in a tanning bed. The receptionist gave Janiah a smile, then ushered her into Pena's office.

Nemesio Pena had a long face and a mane of straight, black hair that danced upon the shoulders of his expensive camel-hair jacket. He reminded Janiah of a younger version of the actor Danny Trejo.

His office was dominated by a U-shaped desk with a desktop computer in one corner of it.

The desk's surface was uncluttered, except for a few papers fanned out in front of his chair. To Janiah, the office did not really feel like it was an actual work site. It had all the qualities of a replica-filled showroom.

Pena came around to greet her. "Hello, Ms. Mack," he said. "Thanks for coming by." He shook Janiah's hand and she noticed him taking a look at her fingers. She figured that he was checking out her blue-tipped French manicure fingernails. She was probably something of a disappointment to him. She did not look particularly dangerous, or anything like Amanda Nunes or Ronda Rousey. Pena was checking to see whether she had the signs of hand conditioning you see in some karate students: enlarged knuckles, calluses. Her shoulders were a bit thick and the muscles in her arms were well-toned, but the only sign of advanced training in her hands was the bulge in the web between her thumb and forefinger that she'd developed from all the knife and stick work with Divine Mathematics.

Pena motioned her to a small sitting area of low chairs and they sat. "It's a pleasure to meet you, Ms. Mack,"

Pena said.

"A pleasure to meet you, also, Mr. Pena," Janiah said in return.

"Please, call me Nemesio," Pena said.

"Okay, then I must insist you call me Janiah," Janiah said with a smile.

"Well, Janiah, I know that you've been training with Divine Mathematics for a little over ten years," Pena said. "I like Fifty-Two Blocks and Divine Mathematics' name… and yours… is well respected in martial arts circles." He smiled. "You know, for a big city, the Atlanta martial arts scene is pretty small."

Janiah nodded. "Seems that way."

"But even though he is respected, I don't hear much about Divine Mathematics," he said. "It would be fantastic to visit his school. He really sounds impressive."

Janiah smiled and nodded again. "I hope I can be of some help to you," she said, changing the subject. "You need some PR pieces done for a martial arts exhibit?"

That got Pena back on track. "Yeah," he said. "Let me show you what we've got planned." He gestured Janiah toward the granite desk.

Pena pushed the fan of papers to one side. "I've managed to get some fantastic blades for this show, he said. "You wouldn't believe what a pain the Chinese, Koreans, Japanese and even the Thai have been about letting this stuff out of the country. The security bond alone is killing me."

He opened a manila file and spread out some papers.

"What I'm putting together, Janiah, is a display of rare swords, machetes, knives and other weapons from all over the world, all of which have a documented association with some of the most famous warriors in martial arts history."

Janiah looked at one sheet of paper. It listed a series of weapon types, descriptions of individual pieces, and estimated value. There were *katana and wakizashi from Japan*; long and short swords from Europe; bolo from the Philippines; iklwa, ida, pinga, and takouba from Africa and katar push daggers from India. The well-crafted weapons would be interesting to any serious martial artist, but what was really fascinating to Janiah were the names of the original owners of the items.

"Wow," she said, looking at the list.

Pena looked pleased. "Wow is right. Some of these pieces are being allowed out of their countries for the first time and every one of them is linked to famous warriors."

He read aloud from the list: "Queen Nzinga, Miyamoto Musashi, William Wallace," he paused significantly, then continued, "Shaka Zulu."

Janiah could feel Pena eyeing her for a reaction. And he got one—Janiah's expression showed that she was amazed and impressed by the collection. She had to admit that the weapons assembled were bound to draw a crowd.

Pena was a bit of an egotist and knew his idea was a brilliant one, but he was also shrewd enough to know what he didn't know. A show like this would have martial artists as well as scholars coming out of the woodwork. A significant number would be fairly well informed. As a result, Pena needed to make sure that his display's hype was historically accurate. He could have tried to get some reputable PR person to do it, but Pena was not really connected with those circles.

President Nix had sensed that Nemesio was rapidly emerging as a successful—and wealthy—entrepreneur in search of some respectability. If Janiah could do Pena a favor on the cheap, the relationship with Nix would grow and everyone would be happy. The college president would give Pena a veneer of respectability. Pena would be slowly courted and stroked and eventually cajoled into making a sizable donation to Spelman.

It was a very finely choreographed dance where need, ego, money, and illusion swirled together.

Janiah's role in the process was pretty straightforward.

Pena called in his receptionist to make copies of the documents in the folder and asked Janiah to come up with some writings on the different historical figures and their role in warrior culture. "Nothing too complicated, now, Janiah," Pena said. "A little blood, a little guts, a little *Black Fists and Afros*." He grinned at Janiah and she felt the urge to grin back. Pena was not her kind of person, but it was hard not to respond to someone who was so obviously having so much fun.

"You ever been to Martial Masters before, Ms. Mack… err, Janiah?"

Janiah shook her head.

Pena headed for the door, giving her a "come along" jerk of his head.

"I've been working on this place for years. Started as a shrine to my Holy Trinity of Martial Arts movies—Bruce Lee, Jackie Chan and Sonny Chiba. I got a sense, though, that this martial arts thing was going to be big. So, over time, I've been adding the memorabilia of other stars and their movies as well as famous martial artists and warriors from around the world. Now I have a gallery for traveling displays."

"A collector's dream," Janiah said.

Pena smiled. "It's a beautiful thing. Check it out."

From the other side of the lobby waterfall, they entered the public area through large oak doors. On this side, instead of an office reception area, there was a rock garden. They walked around it and then accessed the training and exhibition hall. "Some of the stuff on the list is in there right now," Pena said as they walked past the garden. "The rest is on the way. Got a special security detail to watch it."

They walked past the displays of Jet Li, Gordon Liu and Muhammad Ali and went in through a pair of sliding shoji screen doors. The *dojo* behind the doors was bright and airy, with a hardwood floor and tasteful decorations.

Pena watched Janiah as she took a look around.

"Pretty nice, huh?" he said.

"Looks like you've got it all figured out," Janiah said.

Pena grinned again. "You know it. And, as a perk, I get to work out here."

"You still train?" Janiah asked. "What with all the collecting and money making?"

"I try to keep at it," he said with a smirk. "I'm training with this master now; he's incredible."

Pena glanced at his Rolex with the alligator band. "As

a matter of fact, it's about time for my workout. Would you like to watch?"

And on cue, Alfredo Mejia, the man in the Korean general's uniform that had challenged Divine Mathematics, walked into the *dojo*.

In street clothes he looked almost normal, although the tight polo shirt stretched across his torso gave the impression that this was a man who spent a great deal of time lifting weights and looking at himself in the mirror.

Mejia stopped short when he saw them and glared at Janiah for a minute.

"Fred," she said, just to annoy him.

He looked at Pena. "What's going on here, Nemesio?"

Pena did not get where he was by being dense. He looked at Janiah, then at Mejia, and realized that what he had here were two opposing forces in very close proximity. He moved in so that he was at least partly between them. "Ms. Mack is doing some consulting for the museum. I didn't realize you knew each other."

"A brief acquaintance," Janiah said.

Mejia muttered something under his breath. It sounded like "bitch."

Pena did not pick it up. "I had just invited Ms. Mack to watch our workout."

Mejia bristled. "I don't like outsiders watching me train, Nemesio."

Pena looked a bit embarrassed.

Janiah jumped in, "It's okay, Mr. Pena. Maybe some

other time." She held up the file he gave her. "I'll get to work." For a minute, she had the urge to tell him to get someone else for his trainer, but he was hiring her to do some writing, not to manage his affairs.

As she walked out, Pena looked a bit disappointed.

Not half as disappointed as he would have been if I told him the last time I saw Fred Mejia, Divine Mathematics had knocked him out and Fred had peed his pants, she thought.

CHAPTER FOUR

Stone Mountain is located in the city in Georgia named after it. Stone Mountain is not really a mountain, it is actually a quartz monzonite domed hill and the site of Stone Mountain Park. Every morning Janiah ran up to the top of Stone Mountain and down the other side, then ran back to her car. It was almost Summer and it was hot. This day, she was praying for a breeze.

Divine Mathematics was a big believer in running and encouraged all of his students to do so. He insisted that his advanced students stay fit, which meant that running, or weight-lifting, or both was essential.

One of his favorite stories was the one about the brother from Chicago who moved to Osogbo, Nigeria to live out a life-long dream of learning self defense from this Ijakadi master. The brother got there for his first day of training and the master asked him, "What's the best self-defense technique?"

The brother thought about it and proudly said, "To run away."

The old master nodded and said, "Correct." Then, he

added, "So start running. If I catch you, I'm whooping your ass."

Janiah was not sure if the story was true or not but she got the point: a good martial artist needs to stay in shape.

So she ran every day.

As she ran she would think. This day, she thought about Divine Mathematics, the truest, realist martial arts master she had ever met and she had met many in her travels. She had presented herself to him ten years ago, with formal written recommendation from her former teacher—a Black Belt in Brazilian Jujutsu and a former Golden Gloves champion. She had knelt on Divine Mathematics' stone floor and offered him the neatly written letter from her first teacher with both hands. Then she had waited.

She knew a bit about Divine Mathematics, even back then--his prowess in 52 Blocks, his skill as a fighter with or without weapons, his knowledge about African martial arts. Stories about the "brutality" of his training were used to scare cocky black belts from other schools into a type of humility and appreciation for *their* teachers. So when she came before Divine Mathematics that day, she studied him carefully.

He was about the same height as her, below average for a man, and stocky. He did not look like a stereotypical old martial arts master you see in the movies or like an MMA champion, but Divine Mathematics radiated a type of power that you could feel. His hair was cut so short that from a distance he appeared totally bald. His eyes were hard and dark, and the expression on his face was one of total reserve. The fingers of his hands were thick and strong-looking as they reached for the introductions Janiah brought. Divine Mathematics glanced once at her, read the letter, and frowned.

"What's this shit?" he said. "I thought you were bringing me a letter telling me I won a million dollars from Publishing House, or something. Come back tomorrow."

Janiah could not tell whether he was serious or playing around, but when he handed her the letter back and walked back to his office, she knew it was time to go. But, thankfully, she did come back the next day and her training began. She learned that the formal Asian way of "Big I and Little You" did not fly at Black Fists and Afros or at any African martial arts, or Fifty-Two Blocks school.

In the early days of working with him, Janiah despaired of knowing when Divine Mathematics and when he was joking, but over the years, she learned that even when he was joking, he was teaching a valuable lesson. She still was not sure whether it was just that she got more used to his ways, or whether his training was making her more perceptive. But was sure that as she persevered at *Black Fists and Afros*, there were times when she swore she could see a glint of approval or satisfaction in his eyes. And just that hint was enough to keep her going.

In the last few days, there had been a subtle increase in the intensity of training, and that's saying something, but there was a pattern, a flow to the logic of what Divine Mathematics did. The years with him had ingrained the pattern in Janiah. But what they were doing lately seemed somehow out of synch. She could sense it in the nature of his comments to the students, in the stiff set of his back as he stalked the *school* floor. She wondered what Divine Mathematics was up to.

Any *martial arts teacher* is a bit erratic at times—they do it to keep their students on their toes. Part of the mystery of a really good martial arts teacher is the way in which their students are perpetually surprised by things, kept just slightly off balance.

Divine Mathematics was a master of this mystery. An astute student could glean clues of the inner workings of the man from the comments he would make after training. The students would sit, row after row of sweaty men and women in navy blue uniform shirts and blue khaki pants, slowing their breathing and listening to the master. Divine Mathematics would always offer parables that reinforced an important lesson. At the end of training, the students would be so worn out that the mind was extremely open. As a result, the stories and advice were imprinted in their memories in a tremendously vivid way.

But there were no parables lately; no stories or jokes, just gruff admonitions to train harder. In response, each student came back for more training even though training's purpose was a mystery. Janiah drove on in the rhythm of the run, mulling the situation over. There was nothing to be done. Divine Mathematics would reveal his purpose in time... or not. It was his choice. He was the master. Janiah thought about something else.

She had finished up Pena's project. It was not exactly a brain teaser. She Dropboxed the file and e-mailed a copy to him just in case. Now she was waiting for the check somewhat impatiently. She made up a little cadence that kept her mind off the sheer boredom of running: "Rich better have my money." She sung it to the tune of *Bitch Better Have My Money*—not the Rihanna version, the 1991 classic by AMG.

She was at the bottom of the mountain, on the hundredth repetition of her little mantra: "Rich... rich-rich... rich better have my money." It went well with the in and out of her breath. After a while she noticed that she was getting some funny looks. "The shoes. The shoes? It's gotta be the shoes," she sang—she was a fan of old school hip-hop.

Nah, it can't be the running shoes, she thought. *These expensive-ass Mizuno Wave Tenjins better* not *be getting me funny looks.*

She was pretty sure that she had not been singing too loudly. Then she started to pick up the crunch of car tires slowly approaching her as she jogged toward the parking lot.

The unmarked police car came grinding up beside her with the blue lights flashing. The car gave her a quick *bloop* on the siren. She stopped.

There were two of men, and they had that look about them—that "everybody is guilty of something"-look. The driver was a light-skinned Black man with freckles and a short, sandy-brown afro, with a thick police mustache. The other man had a smooth, medium-brown complexion and strong, handsome features. His hair was styled in a low fade. They were both dressed in white cotton shirts and loosened ties. Janiah peeked in the back of the *Dodge Charger*. Their sports jackets were neatly folded in the backseat, and the floors were cluttered with paper wrappers and empty coffee cups.

The driver's window rolled down.

"What seems to be the problem, Officer?" Janiah said.

The driver eyed her silently then looked at the man with him. "She seems nervous."

"You know Black folks get nervous around the

police," the man with the low fade said.

The one with freckles continued, "Ms. Mack?" She looked at the one with the low fade then nodded.

"We're looking for some information. Could you come with us, please?" The driver asked.

"I need to see some badges and ID, first," Janiah said.

The driver made a show of patting himself absently and muttered, "Damn... I thought I had 'em. I must have left them at the strip club we just left."

His partner smiled at Janiah and said, "I must have left mine at your mama's house."

Both men laughed.

"Hop in," the one in the passenger's seat said.

"You want me up front or in the nasty backseat?" Janiah asked. The sweat was beginning to bead on her forehead and run down her face now that she had stopped running.

"You sit next to me, Ronda Rousey," the driver said.

"I'm a sister," Janiah said. "Find a Black woman MMA fighter to compare me to."

"Ronda Rousey is Black," the driver said. "Her mother is a fourth Black and she's an eighth."

"An eighth... really?" Janiah said with a smirk.

"Hey... one drop, remember?"

"Whatever," Janiah said.

The man with the low fade got out, eased the jackets over and settled into the backseat. The jackets looked clean and pressed. They were the only tidy thing in the vehicle.

Janiah got in, bumping her knee on the radio console mounted on the dashboard, and they rolled slowly around the parking lot until they could exit and then they headed back onto the streets. No one said anything. The radio made soft squawks.

Janiah asked if she could roll down my window. The driver rolled it down with the power console on his left. She turned to look over her shoulder at the man sitting behind her.

"So Tony," she said. "How's Mama?"

"She's good," Tony said. "Wants me to give up being an investigative journalist and take over Daddy's church."

"You know Mama," Janiah said. "It was her dream that you be a bigger preacher than Daddy—one of those TV evangelists—not a reporter for Fox News."

"I'm not even a Christian," Tony said. "Besides, I love my job."

"You could at least be on camera reporting the news, you're handsome," Janiah said.

"Thanks, sis," Tony said. "But being in front of the camera is your thing. Finding the facts and putting together information and evidence to get to the truth… that's my thing."

"At heart, he's a detective, like his boy," the driver said, pointing a thumb at himself.

"When we were children, you used to say you wanted

to own a video store," Janiah said to the driver. "What happened to that dream, James?"

"Umm... technology," James replied. "Do you see any Blockbusters anywhere? Any Hollywood Video? DVDs are old school now."

"But you became a pig, of all things?" Janiah said. "You used to hate the police."

"Still do," James said. "But this way, I get to be the Spook Who Sat By the Door on these white folks' asses."

"Let me know how that works out for you," Janiah said.

James Pedersen was a movie buff, and had developed an annoying habit of recycling old lines of film dialogue and movie titles into his conversation. Tony and Janiah were used to it.

"What have you been up to, Chef Boyardee?" Tony asked.

Janiah sighed. *It's gonna be a long day*, she thought.

CHAPTER FIVE

"Nothing much," she replied to Tony. "The show... working out... training."

They drove on the I-20, heading west. Neither James nor Tony said much. One was Janiah's big brother, and James had been his best friend for thirty years, so he was no stranger to her, but she wasn't getting any information from either of them. They rode in silence.

"You're a chatterbox today, Tony," Janiah said.

"Yeah," he said. Then he began to grope around for a *Newport* cigarette.

"Don't smoke that cancer stick in my car, T," James said. James had quit about two years ago and was slowly, inexorably, forcing Tony into doing the same.

"Come on, bruh," Tony said.

"*Come on,* what, join you in chemo?" James said.

"Asshole," Tony mumbled.

It's like listening to an old married couple, Janiah thought. *But Tony didn't light up, though.* She chuckled.

They also didn't say much about why they were now heading up Ponce De Leon Avenue.

Eventually, however, the stop and go of city traffic seemed to shake something out of them.

"Still doing that 'African Karate' stuff?" James asked.

Janiah grinned. "Yeah," she said. "And it's Fifty-Blocks and Ijakadi; nothing to do with and nothing like karate."

Tony snorted. "You can't drop kick a sniper on a rooftop or dodge a bullet with *any* of that martial art shit."

"The trick is to not be where the sniper or the bullet is," Janiah said. "Avoidance is the highest level of martial arts."

"What's this I hear about you working for Nemesio Pena?" James chimed in.

"That's true," Janiah replied. "How did you find that out?"

James swerved around a pickup truck that shot across two lanes without warning. He cursed under his breath then asked, "You read the paper this morning, Janiah?"

"No. Why?" Janiah said.

Tony rooted around in the trash in the back of the car and came up with a copy of the *Atlanta Journal-Constitution*. He slapped it between Janiah and James and said, "Check it out, sis."

The headline read "Kung Fu Killer." The crux of the article was about homicide. Early that morning, Mr.

Nemesio Pena, noted entrepreneur, had gone to his Martial Masters museum for a scheduled early appointment with his personal trainer. The trainer, identified as Alfredo Mejia, a martial arts expert, had been found in Martial Masters' performance space, dead of an apparent broken neck. While the Atlanta Police Department was still investigating the cause of death, the *Atlanta Journal-Constitution* speculated it was caused by a "karate chop." Theft did not appear to have been a motive for the killing and the investigation was ongoing.

"Oh," Janiah said. "A karate chop. That's the reason for this visit. Nemesio Pena turn me in, y'all?"

"Look, Janiah," Tony said. "James and I both need to get ahead of this—him for the case; me for the scoop, so we have to talk to you for a little bit." Tony wasn't exactly apologetic. If it bothered him at all to pick up his own sister for questioning, it didn't show. *Just doing his stupid job*, Janiah thought.

"Come on, Tony," Janiah chuckled. "You don't seriously think I'm a suspect."

Tony held up a calming hand. James, however, wasn't going to let it go. "Pena likes you for it," he said.

The car fell silent.

"Here's what we've got, Janiah," James finally went on. "The esteemed Mr. Pena gets a call from his janitorial staff early this A.M. to hightail it to his office. By the time he gets there, the uniforms are on the scene stretching yellow tape. Old Nemesio takes a good look around… pokes about in his office. Then he goes over to the museum. He takes one good look and that about does it."

"You mean he said I did it?" Janiah asked

skeptically.

"First he had to stop throwing up," James replied. "Then he got cleaned up and started talking. And—"

"Presto," Tony chimed in. "Your name pops up."

I looked from one to the other and couldn't think of a thing to say.

"Here's what we've got, Janiah..." James went on. "You doing a job for Nemesio Pena... Mejia in the mix.... the two of you have some sort of confrontation, some sort of mysterious martial arts stuff... Mejia tells Pena about it... a day or so later, Mejia turns up dead. So—"

"So, we've got Nemesio Pena babbling about some karate-to-the-death grudge match," Tony said. "I personally think it's bullshit, but—"

"Motive," James said.

"Then we got all this 'death touch' hype. You should read Atlanta Daily World's version."

"So now, Ms. Martial Arts Expert, we got the means," James sound.

"You do anything last night, Janiah? Out with friends? A date?" Tony asked.

"No," Janiah said. She got a sinking feeling as Tony ran down the list of possibilities, trying to see whether she had an alibi. "I stayed in and wrote recipes."

"Phone calls?" Tony asked.

She shook her head.

"And," James said with a flourish, "opportunity."

They came to a halt in front of the Martial Masters museum. There was a police cruiser on the scene and a uniformed cop by the door.

"Hey, come on. Y'all can't be serious," Janiah protested.

James let out a long sigh. He put a cardboard sign with an APD sticker on the dash and turned the car's engine off.

"Nah," Tony said. "If I thought that, I wouldn't be helping James establish a case against my little sister."

"You'll have to make a statement, though," James said. "Give some prints, that sort of thing."

"But what we really want is some advice on this one," Tony said as he climbed out of the backseat.

The three of them stood for a minute, looking at the front of Martial Masters, the chrome and granite building looked no worse for wear and the business of the city flowed past it as if nothing had happened there. But the police were coming and going. Thirty minutes ago, Janiah was running up and down Stone Mountain. Now she was in a very different world. Forensic experts in white jumpsuits were taking out little plastic bags with items in them. Radios garbled and cops stood around drinking coffee.

Janiah's T-shirt had dried and her legs had that "good ache" feel from the run. She stood there, in her expensive running shoes, feeling fit and strong, but it didn't do much for her confidence at the moment.

Tony tapped her lightly on the shoulder and took her by the arm. "Don't worry," he said quietly. "It'll be okay."

"Besides, if anybody tried to take you in, you'd kill

'em with your *ninja* death touch," James said.

Janiah threw up her fingers before her like the claws of a praying mantis and held one knee up above her waist.

James shook his head. "Come on, Karate Kid," he said as they walked toward the door. "You ever been on a crime scene, Janiah?"

"No," she replied.

"One rule," James said.

"Okay," Janiah said, looking over at him.

"Don't touch anything," he said

They walked in, passing the uniformed cop, whose eyes briefly refocused as they approached, but glazed over once James flashed his badge.

Plastic yellow crime scene tape was strung across the entrance to the museum that Nemesio Pena had showed Janiah with such pride the other day. Inside the museum, the room was empty. Janiah let out a deep breath, realizing that she had been holding her breath in anticipation of having to see the corpse.

But it was long gone. There was only the taped outline of Mejia's body on the floor, but that was it other than small pieces of paper and tape laying around—the detritus of the crime scene investigators—but not much else.

Then she saw the wall. She did a double take then moved toward the wall slowly and read what was written there, apparently scrawled with a thick magic marker. She had seen the characters before, tattooed on the arm of a drunk white woman that had spilled a drink on her at the party after the Shorty Awards, which honor the best of social media, a couple of years ago. The woman had turned to her and said, "Watch it nig—" and Janiah had knocked her out before the woman could finish her sentence.

Janiah had gone home and researched the meaning of the tattoo on the white woman's arm.

"Oh, man," she murmured.

"You know what that means, Janiah?" Tony asked.

She turned to look at them. "Yes."

"We're assuming whoever got in here and deaded Mejia did it," James said.

"What's it say?" They asked in unison.

Janiah looked from one man to the other. A uniformed cop drifted closer to eavesdrop. "Let's get a cup of coffee," she said.

They ended up in a diner, hunched over the table in a booth near the back. The waitress wandered over, a Pyrex carafe in hand, and filled their cups.

"Thanks, that's it," James said to the waitress. She looked disappointed that he didn't ask for donuts, but James refused to give in to the stereotype.

Then the men sat there and simply looked at her, waiting.

"That message on the wall—Roa—is white supremacist lingo," she said. "It means, 'Race over all.'"

"So some Proud Boy or Alt-Wrong is behind this," Tony said.

"Could be the fool's last name," James said.

"Have you ever met anybody with the name Roa?" Janiah asked. "Have you ever even heard of somebody with that name?"

James shrugged.

"But what clinches it is the number written under 'Roa'," Janiah said. "1488. In white supremacist lingo, 1488 is a combination of two popular white supremacist numeric symbols—the first symbol is fourteen, which is shorthand for a fourteen word-long slogan: 'We must secure the existence of our people and a future for white children.' The second is eighty-eight, which stands for 'Heil Hitler', because H is the eighth letter of the alphabet. Together, the numbers form a general endorsement of white supremacy and its beliefs."

"Who comes up with this shit?" James said.

"A redneck with too much time on his hands," Tony said.

"Actually, '1488' was created by David Lane in the early 1990s, the founder of *Wotansvolk*, a form of white nationalist paganism," Janiah said. "Wotansvolk has survival of the Aryan race as its core and trains for and plans white revolution. When I researched the chick's tattoo, it sent me down a rabbit hole of interesting, and scary, information."

"So, what's that got to do with offing this Mejia dude?" Tony asked.

"Hey, James is the detective and you're the investigative journalist," Janiah countered. "So detect... investigate."

"What we have here is a murder in a museum specializing in all that martial arts stuff you do," James said.

"The victim appears to have been done in without an apparent weapon," Tony added. "Now, the Alt-Writing on the wall… what's that all about?"

"People who sign their work want to be known," James replied. "Even if they sign with an alias."

"You don't think this was just a robbery gone bad?" Janiah asked.

"Janiah," Tony began slowly, as if he was talking to a simpleton."Somebody breaks into a martial arts museum and takes what… nunchuks?"

"You don't bypass an electronic alarm system in midtown, go through all that planning, murder somebody, and take nothing of any real value," James chimed in." He consulted his notes and quoted, "A personal inventory by Mr. Pena confirms nothing missing except an old wooden sword that formed a minor part of the display."

"No thief is gonna act like that," Tony said." Pena has a safe in his office with over fifty K in it and it was left untouched." Tony shook his head and frowned, seemingly outraged by Janiah's ineptness.

She sat, digesting this.

"And, if something goes wrong and you do have to bust somebody's head to the white meat, you tend to haul ass up outta there quick," James said. "Your basic thief doesn't whip out a Sharpie and write esoteric symbols and shit before stuffing valuables into a sack."

"So what do you mean? What happened?" Janiah

asked.

"This wasn't a smash and grab sort of thing," Tony said.

"Maybe just a smash," James said.

Janiah figured he had seen the body before they came to fetch her.

"This is some weird murder," Tony said. "And that '*1488*' shit is the clue."

"A guy like this is gonna leave a trail," James said. "And a trail—"

"Is all two Nancy Drew-Luther dudes like y'all need," Janiah said.

"Exactly," Tony said.

"Who in the hell is Nancy Drew?" James asked.

"I'll buy you one of her books for your birthday," Tony said.

"Cool," James said.

Janiah shook her head.

They drained their cups of coffee and headed out. Tony paid the cashier, and James provided a running commentary as they headed out to the car, which was double-parked out front.

"We'll run a check, Janiah," James said. "We'll need a statement from you. Compare your prints with any latents the lab picked up. They won't match and you'll be cleared. Then, we'll see if there are reports with similar MOs. Shouldn't be hard to spot. The newspaper clippings alone should stick out a mile."

"Martial Mayhem," Tony said.

"Judo Justice," James chimed in. "Some shit like that."

And off they went. This time, Janiah had to sit in the back.

CHAPTER SIX

When James invited Janiah back to his squad room, she had all those B-movie images of where police work lodged in her brain—dark and dingy rooms crammed with untidy desks, choked with cigarette smoke, and smelling of old coffee and stale sweat.

In reality, James had a desk behind a cubicle in a brightly lit, capacious room made mazelike by portable half-walls that divided up the space. Phones didn't ring; they beeped and each desk had a state-of-the-art laptop on it. A *Keurig* coffee maker was in plain view, along with prominently displayed "No Smoking" signs.

They're hi-tech beating our asses now, Janiah thought.

Despite most of her stereotypes being debunked, there were some that proved true. The room was littered with coffee cups—anonymous, cheap Styrofoam ones, others from Starbucks, and even several ceramic mugs near the Keurig. There were also two or three empty boxes from *Krispy Kreme*.

The surface illusion of order and neatness was

somewhat damaged when Tony escorted Janiah to James' cubicle. Cartons filled with folders and dog-eared documents were shoved beneath his desk. Little slips of paper were tucked under blotters, half-empty coffee cups, and anything else remotely heavy.

James was on the phone. He stood up and peered over the wall that divided him from Tony and Janiah, murmuring "Uh huh, uh huh," into the receiver and taking notes. James' pen ran out of ink. He grimaced and snapped his fingers at Tony while throwing his dead pen in the trash. Tony pulled a pen from the interior pocket of his blazer then tossed it to James.

James sat down, rolled his chair out, and swiveled in it to eye Janiah briefly. Tony pulled some paperwork off a chair and gestured for her to sit. James hung up the phone.

Janiah eyed him expectantly.

"Nah," James said, shaking his head. "Nothing. That was a different case."

He thumbed through some pages of notes in a little book. James had thick, freckled hands and his fingers made the book look tiny. "Okay," he said. "Janiah, your landlady confirms your statement that you were home the night of the murder. She heard you come in and various noises in the apartment for most of the evening. Seems to corroborate your statement."

Tony raised an eyebrow. "Noises? Aight now, sis."

"Don't get excited, T, it's a two-family house. I live upstairs and the floors creak."

"Yeah, creaky floors," Tony said rolling his eyes. "We'll go with that."

"I'm glad you were home knocking boots, Janiah," James said. "Because there's a shitload of other stuff for me to wade through here."

Janiah sighed and placed a palm to her forehead. "I wasn't knocking—" She decided not to explain herself to them. "Wait... you've got something?"

Tony and James swung their chairs to face Janiah at almost exactly the same time. She felt left out because her chair had no wheels. Then they looked at each other.

"To the Bat-Cave," James said.

Janiah followed them out of the cubicle and into a conference room.

It had only been a few days since Mejia's murder, but in that short time, the investigation's paperwork had ballooned. James hauled in various boxes, manila envelopes, files, and plugged a cell phone into the huge television on the wall of the Bat-Cave. The conference room was carpeted with a computer also hooked up to the television, and in the center of the room was a large oval table with plush brown leather chairs. Tony and James dumped the stuff at one end and began sorting through it.

Janiah sat and watched the process, waiting until they were ready. Finally, James pressed a button on the phone and the television screen came to life. On the screen was some police officer narrating the examination of the crime scene, identifying the location, the hour and day, and the fact that James was the investigating officer.

The camera panned carefully around the room, noting entrances, windows, lighting and alarm controls, orienting the viewer. Then it carefully focused on the floor where Mejia lay.

The camera panned over the body. Mejia's form was like something discarded. It had the shape and dimension of a human being, but it was just lying there in a heap, without any of the sense of connection you get from looking at a person at rest. Mejia's left shoulder looked droopy and it was obvious from his face that Mejia had taken a major blow to the head. What looked like an oak sword was pinned under the body.

James shoved some still photos across the table: Mejia from various angles. "Okay," he began. "So much for streaming. Alfredo Mejia, aged forty-two. Casual employee of Martial Masters museum. Ran a martial arts school in Little Five Points. Did some minor stuff as a juvenile, but nothing on his record for the last twenty years or so."

"No apparent problems in his life that would suggest he was anything but a dude who was in the wrong place at the wrong time," Tony said.

"We put an end to that grudge match thing, by the way," James said. "Once we squeezed Pena, we got to the bottom of it. Anyway, we told him that you're clean."

"What was his reaction?" Janiah asked.

"He seemed like his mind was on other things," James said. "He did say that he never really thought it was you; you seemed okay."

"Whatever," Janiah said, rolling her eyes. "I seemed so okay he couldn't wait to finger me for murder."

James waved it away. "It happens." Then he picked up a piece of paper and read from it, "Time of death is estimated somewhere between two-thirty and six-thirty A.M."

"Is that significant?" Janiah asked.

"There's a four-hour margin of error in this stuff," Tony said. "He was found at around seven-thirty in the morning, so it doesn't tell us much that we didn't already know."

"Deceased suffered a number of fractures, including a cranial blow that might have killed him," James continued.

"Do you know what cracked his skull?" Janiah was trying to remain as calm as they were, but her eyes kept drifting to the frozen video and the stills on the table.

"Cellulose fragments from his shirt and scalp suggest the weapon was wood of some type; we haven't got it fixed yet."

"Let me ask," I said. "Mejia suffered a fractured collarbone?"

They nodded.

"The head wound is obvious. Any sign of damage to the right wrist or forearm?"

Tony consulted the M.E.'s report. "No breaks that are noted. Did seem to have taken some bangs there, though."

Janiah got up and shut the TV off so she could concentrate better.

"Okay," she continued. "So Fred Mejia is in Martial Masters guarding Nemesio Pena's exhibit. He got let in when?"

"Building shuts down about eleven. Lobby security logged the cleaners out and Mejia in at ten P.M. Mejia activated the Martial Masters alarm and buttoned up for the night. There's no lobby security presence until five-thirty A.M."

"Custodial shift comes in at seven," James said. "Secretary at seven-thirty. She takes a quick look in the museum and all hell breaks loose."

"She screamed so loud, the guards spilled their coffee," Tony said. "They were very upset."

"So how'd the murderer get in?" Janiah asked.

Tony snorted. "That's the easy part."

"Yeah," James said. "Mejia let him in."

Mejia lay sprawled there in the photo with head wounds and offered no clue to Janiah as to why he let his killer in.

"What we need to know is whether you've got any insights into what happened," Tony said.

She nodded. "This thing wedged under the body, do you have it?"

"Sure." James pulled another photo out of an envelope. It was a *bokken*—a Japanese wooden sword used for training. It's usually the size and shape of a katana, or samurai sword.

"Murder weapon?" Janiah asked.

"Nah," James said. "We're pretty certain it was Mejia's weapon."

"What makes you so sure?" Janiah asked.

"He carved his initials in the butt end." James said.

"Then again," Tony began, "the letters could stand

for 'Ass Master."

"Anti Mexican," James suggested.

"Makes sense," Tony said. "He was Cuban. It could mean Ape-Man, though."

Janiah cut them off in mid-flow, "One of his students can probably identify it as Mejia's."

They seemed somewhat put out, and just stared at her.

James shook his head and went on. "We're looking at fragments in his wounds. We can't place the wood's type yet."

"The wood of the murder weapon could be a lot of things," Janiah said. "Those wood fragments look like oak. You can also have the forensic guys check hickory. It's commonly used to make *bokken*. If they really want to get exotic, they can try loquat."

James looked at Tony and silently mouthed "Loquat?" Tony shrugged.

"The wounds seem fairly consistent with the kind of damage you might get if two people went at each other with wooden swords," Janiah said.

"How'd you figure the collarbone break?" James asked.

"You can see a little extra slump in Mejia's shoulder," she pointed out, spreading the different still shots out and pointing it out in each picture. "It's also a pretty easy bone to snap if you hit it right.

"Charming," Tony said.

"Yeah, well, it's a common attack," Janiah said. "And if you do it with a blade, you can almost cut somebody in half. With a wooden sword, you would most probably break the clavicle. Now, if Mejia also had sustained some damage to his right wrist, he would have a hard time using the sword. Japanese and Korean stylists need two hands to use their swords well. With his clavicle busted, Mejia would have been in big trouble. You could use a real blade one-handed, but a bokken wouldn't be very effective."

"So what are you saying?" Tony asked.

"I think Mejia had a duel with someone using a wooden weapon. The murderer could have been using a sword or a staff or a bunch of other weapons, but the murderer definitely has some training."

"A duel?" James grimaced.

The light went on in Tony's head. He pointed at James, snapping his fingers. "Sure, sure. Nemesio Pena wasn't too far off the mark. Mejia sets it up ahead of time, lets the guy in for the big showdown. Otherwise, why carry around a wooden sword?"

James nodded. "Maybe." He looked at Janiah. "This Mejia know what he was doing?"

Janiah nodded.

"Okay, so he's no karate-virgin," James said. He thought a bit and said, almost to himself, "Been around the block a few times. Knows the cardinal rule of weapons."

"What's that?" Janiah asked, curious.

"Never bring a knife to a gun fight," James replied. "So, if Mejia's carrying a stick—"

"It's a *bokken*," Janiah said, correcting him. "Wooden sword."

"Yeah, whatever," James said. "Then it must have been on purpose. Mejia knew someone was coming and he knew he would need the sword."

"But, he got in over his head," Tony said.

"What's the motive, though?" James asked.

"Man, I'd be a lot happier if we had a theft here," Tony said.

"Yeah," James said with a nod. "But if it was just a smash and grab, the whole wooden sword thing would be elaborate as hell."

"I thought we agreed robbery wasn't the motive," Janiah suggested.

Tony and James turned to look at her.

"What you tend to find, Janiah," James said, "is that motives tend to be a mishmash of things."

She shrugged and went on. "Maybe here, the duel itself was the murderer's real interest. This wasn't a robbery scheme that didn't come off. Maybe the killer got what he came for."

They chewed on that quietly for a minute. Then James looked at Tony. "Mack, your people are weird."

"Look," I said, "whoever did this was trained. From what I hear, Mejia was pretty good."

Tony looked toward the photos. "Not as good as he thought he was."

"No one's as good as they think they are," James said.

James has never met Divine Mathematics, Janiah thought.

"Besides, if somebody used Mejia to get into the Martial Masters museum to rob it and then planned on killing him, don't you think they would have brought something fairly lethal along?" Janiah asked.

"Looks like they did," James said. He had a point. One way or the other, the man was dead.

"I mean that they would have brought a *real* weapon, James, not a wooden replica. With these things, you're essentially bludgeoning somebody to death. Look at him lying there."

They both eyed the photos.

"Mejia was an expert. If you had your choice, would you go three rounds with him?"

Tony shook his head. "Not even on a good day. In my prime."

James laughed. "Like you ever had a prime."

"Seriously, y'all," Janiah said.

"Nah, you're right," James said, his eyes narrowing as he sat and thought. "A typical MO would be to gain access in the middle of the night, get the stuff, and then *pow*... a nine-millimeter shot to the back of Mejia's head. Simple."

"A little hard on the carpet, though," Tony said.

The two men exchanged glances, suddenly aware of

new possibilities.

"If theft was the primary motive, the methodology would be what?" Janiah asked.

"Get in and get out," Tony said.

James jumped in. "But here, the person of interest chooses a time when someone's around. And there's this duel." He looked at Janiah. "The M.E.'s report says this guy took a hell of a beating. How long do you think it took?"

"It's hard to say," Janiah commented. "Theoretically, it could have been over quickly. It depends on the skill levels involved."

"Was Mejia highly skilled?" James asked.

"He was pretty good," Janiah said.

"Lots of bruising on the arms and torso," James said. "Looks like the victim put up quite a fight. So this didn't go down quickly." He paused and looked down at some of the still photos. Then he fished out a sheet of paper. "Here's the report from the shrink liaison." He glanced at Janiah and answered the look on her face. "We got a revolving group of forensic psychiatrists on call. You get a murder like this, we use 'em for profiling."

"Any good?" Janiah asked them.

James squinted and looked at the wall like he was focusing on something in the distance. "Depends on the case," he said noncommittally. "What we have here, the good doctor concludes, is an elaborate killing. It took some time. It was carefully thought out and carefully executed."

"Nice pun," Tony said.

James didn't rise to the bait. He just droned on: "The doctor says, 'the elaborate methodology, the apparent absence of other motives, the almost… ritual staging. While the identity of the killer cannot be determined, the profile is a male, between the ages of twenty-one and forty'." He looked up at Janiah. "This is the profile of most murderers, Janiah. So far, these guys aren't impressing me." He scanned the next sheet. "Ooh, wait, there's more. 'The killer is intelligent, probably highly so—'"

"Unlike the writer of that report," Tony snickered.

"The doc goes on to say, 'he doesn't stand out in a crowd. He's quiet, polite, even affable'."

Janiah looked from one man to the other to get their reaction. They looked like they had heard it all before.

"Aha!" James said. "Here it is… 'Somewhere in this man's past… in his childhood… behaviors of this type generated as a response to a life event… systematic abuse of some sort… often sexual.'"

"Thank God they got that in. I was beginning to worry," Tony said.

"There's more, Tony," James said. "Lemme see… 'Deep-seated feeling of insecurity spawns a pathological need to exert control. The more intense the need, the greater the response.'" He looked up again. "These jokers cream their jeans over serial killers."

"I sort of get that impression," Janiah said.

"Which is all well and good," Tony said. "But every time I visit the morgue, I got shrinks spinning these theories about bed-wetting psychos. Know what? Most of the time, the person who put the stiff in the cooler is a friend or a family member, drunk or strung out. You know most murderers, Janiah, they're not Dylann Roof or Lizzie Borden. They're people who made bad choices, or got their buttons pushed one too many times, or just took it a little too far."

"You gotta admit the duel thing is a little nuts, Tony," James said.

"Maybe so. But when it was all over, somebody was still getting zipped into a rubber bag."

That seemed to sum up the situation nicely.

The door opened and another detective stuck his head in "Oh. There you are. James, a call for you from Riverdale."

"Who is it?" James asked.

"Some detective in New Orleans PD homicide named Gregoire. Know her?" James shook his head no. "Well, she says you'll want to talk to her."

"Can you transfer it in here?"

The detective looked offended. "Like I don't have anything to do but hunt you two fools down," he said as the door closed.

"Thanks, Winston," James called.

Eventually, the phone still connected to the television buzzed. James answered, which was how we heard about the Wulff murder.

Detective Sophia Gregoire, NOPD, gave a recital that was disengaged and clinical in that way cops have. James had her on speakerphone and the voice sounded like that of a bored guard coming from somewhere way in the back of a warehouse.

"Pederson? I got the message you posted," she began.

Tony looked like he was going to ask something; James shook his head silently.

"You asked for anything we might have in the files—" she said.

"Martial arts related." James said.

"Bruh," Detective Gregoire said, "this is New Orleans. I got freaks in ninja suits falling out of trees."

"The Big Easy is like another world," James said.

"Maybe not," Gregoire said. "You also mentioned a crime scene with some sort of writing on the wall left as a message."

James sat up a little straighter in his hi-tech chair. "What've you got?" he asked.

"Eight days ago, some German kung-fu instructor gets the shit ripped out of him with a jagged stick. Also '1488' written on the wall. In blood."

"You know what it means?" James asked.

"Oh, yeah. One of the meat wagon guys is up on this kind of stuff. It was some white supremacist shit. Let me find it."

"Bingo," James said. "No need; we got it. Where'd you go with the case?"

"The usual," Gregoire replied. "Rousted some members of the KKK, Evropa and the Proud Boys. Talked with the deceased's family, friends, business associates—"

"And?" James asked.

"And nada," Gregoire replied. "Nothing. Zip. The guy was a straight arrow. The white supremacists didn't know him. No problems we could find, and we turned over all the rocks. Dead end so far."

"Tough," James said without much conviction. They were both professionals and they had a pretty realistic feel for what was solvable and what wasn't.

"Yeah," Gregoire continued. "Look, if you're interested in my notes and some crime scene shots, I can get 'em to you. Then her voice lowered to a whisper. "Look. Pedersen?"

"Yeah."

"You turn up anything, let me know. This was my squeal, but it's on the way to the cold case file, ya know?"

Gregoire hung up.

"What gives, James?" Tony said.

"I got on this secure site for homicide divisions, and I sent out a description of what our case looks like and asked whether anyone had seen anything like it."

"So now, this Detective Gregoire tells us that we've got a similar type of murder taking place a few days ago almost five hundred miles away," Janiah said.

James nodded.

Tony was standing and looking at the crime scene photos. "This thing," he said, "is getting interesting."

"Just one thing, Janiah," James said.

"What?"

"It's still an open case in New Orleans," James replied. "Don't let Nemesio Pena know what's up with the NOPD."

CHAPTER SEVEN

Divine Mathematics couldn't stand it anymore. "Step to him," he shouted, as he churned across the floor toward us. "Step... to... him!"

The early morning training session is not heavily attended. Only the hard core tend to make it. As a result, Divine Mathematics is usually a bit more approachable during this time.

But not this morning. It wasn't a lack of focus, but he seemed preoccupied. Divine Mathematics' perception was normally ratcheted up way above that of normal people. On days like today, he would stare off into the distance and seem frozen with effort, straining to identify the hint of something that was beyond the threshold of his students to sense.

The nonverbal elements of communication and perception are highly valued by African martial arts masters. They prize their ability to grasp the essence of people and things using methods those with less skill can only guess at. Divine Mathematics called such a person "Omoluabi"—*a child born by the Chief of Good Character.* An Omoluabi signified intelligence, truthfulness, mastery of the spoken word, courage, hard work, humility and respect.

Divine Mathematics definitely had and displayed all those qualities. Being Omoluabi enabled Divine Mathematics to touch hand—or cross machetes—with a complete stranger and know the skill level of his opponent before they had begun to do battle.

One could argue that Divine Mathematics' uncanny abilities had to do with subtle physical clues people give off: a look in the eye, their posture, their breathing. The longer Janiah trained the more she knew there was more to it than that.

On days when he was really cooking with gas, it seemed as if Divine Mathematics could actually read people's minds. What scared Janiah most—and everyone else that knew him—was not that Divine Mathematics knew what you were going to do even before you did. That was scary, but it was scarier that he did it by getting inside you somehow.

The feeling was a weird, emotive certainty that washed up from the base of your neck and crept over your scalp. It was often totally unexpected. And distracting.

Janiah knew her teacher too well to think that his mood that day was fueled by anything but that sensation. She had seen it before. It was something he and she did not speak about.

Janiah had been working with one of the more promising junior students. They had been going at it pretty hard and, although the late May morning was not actually hot yet, they were both sweating and constantly adjusting the grip on their weapons. He had a training machete—steel, but with a dulled edge. Janiah was using an African walking stick made of mahogany, which, at about forty inches in length, gave her a bit of a reach over the machete.

The student, whom Divine Mathematics' students called "Silver"—as in *Silverback*, because, like the gorilla, he was big, fast, agile and strong—had come to *Black Fists and Afros* from one of the better escrima schools in the area. As a result, he had amazing reflexes, and he was deadly with a machete or knife, which was why Janiah was using the walking stick.

Far off, just on the edge of her attention, Janiah could hear the sounds of another busy Atlanta Saturday morning starting. She caught herself drifting and refocused on the task at hand—evading a flurry of strikes from Silver that came a bit too close. She knocked aside a thrust toward her chest with the tail end of her stick then tapped Silver on the side of the head with the geodesic dome-shaped head of her weapon.

And then Divine Mathematics blew in like a tornado.

"Mack," he shouted. "What are you doing?"

"I had him, Teacher."

"You *had* him?" he echoed incredulously.

"Yes, sir, she replied. "Head tap."

Divine Mathematics took a glance at Silver, who was wisely not getting anywhere near the conversation.

"Mack," Divine Mathematics sighed. "Look at Silver. Does he look like he's been… had?"

Silver looked like a large onyx statue in a t-shirt and blue cargo pants. When Divine Mathematics turned to face Janiah, Silver gave her a mocking grin behind the teacher's back.

"No, sir," she answered.

"You gotta take the opportunity when it comes," Divine Mathematics said. "More focus, Mack. More spirit. Step to him. Like this."

Divine Mathematics suddenly jerked his whole body toward Silver. He didn't really do anything—he wasn't carrying a weapon and didn't even raise his hands—but the force of Divine Mathematics' presence made Silver step back in alarm.

"Got it?" He looked from me to Silver and back again, motioning us to continue.

We began again while Divine Mathematics glided across the floor, the soles of his Chuck Taylors thumping along the mat. As he headed toward some other trainees he called out to me, but looked at the ceiling, "And step to him!"

It made the rest of that morning pretty interesting for both Silver and Janiah.

Afterward, Divine Mathematics brought Janiah up to the living quarters he had above *Black Fists and Afros*. He wanted to talk.

This was not a common thing with teacher. Janiah had only been to his living quarters twice in all the years that she had known him. But she had mentioned the fact that she was helping out Tony and James with the investigation of the Mejia murder. The martial arts community was buzzing about it. Janiah imagined that her teacher would be deeply concerned, but Divine Mathematics' reaction to her involvement was odd. It involved a hard narrowing of the eyes and a set of the mouth that told her he had displeased him in some way that she could not fathom.

But when she followed him upstairs, she did not say much right away. She sat down and waited while Divine Mathematics fussed in the kitchen making coffee. Divine Mathematics was a coffee fanatic. A couple of years ago, he had won a thirty-day supply of gingerbread latte and caramel macchiato espressos and it was all over for the teacher. Now he was a connoisseur of cappuccinos, lattes, breves, and macchiatos. His kitchen was cluttered with mugs, a coffee maker, an espresso maker, and, his latest addition, a little white ceramic canister to hold his gourmet grounds.

Then, surrounded by the rich aroma of coffee and steamed milk, they sat and Janiah filled Divine Mathematics in on the 1488 case. He listened attentively, with the very intense focus he brought to things in general. But once again, Janiah picked up a sense of agitation and displeasure from him. It was subtle and fleeting, yet there nonetheless.

He nodded when she was done talking, blinked, and said, "Now, Mack. This morning showed something you need to pay attention to. The need for initiative and follow-through."

"Teacher," she protested, "Silver knew that I got him."

Divine Mathematics sipped appreciatively at his mug, then grinned. "Nope," he said. "*You* knew that you got him. Silver didn't."

Janiah started to reply but her teacher held up an open hand in admonition. "Mack. I understand that you're at a point when you can anticipate what would happen and don't feel the need to follow through, right?"

Janiah nodded.

"You gotta remember," he went on. "In combat, two people are involved. Both are very sure that they are better than their opponent. Each thinks he will defeat the other. It's a delusion, of course, but a necessary one for a warrior."

His eyes locked on Janiah, even as he sipped from his mug. "In combat, you gotta shatter your opponent's confidence. You gotta project your spirit in such a way as to let the other one know he's defeated. You can't wait for him to act. You gotta take the initiative… take it to him"

"I know that, Teacher, but in training—"

"The way you train is the way you fight," Divine Mathematics said. "You think you're being righteous, permitting the other person to develop their skills. I understand. But you're really holding yourself back and letting the other person exist in a fantasy world.

"Look." He walked to the wall where his ada rested upon a polished iron holder. The long, broad sword was elegantly simple, steel with the cutting edge on the inside, unlike Asian blades with the cutting edge on the outside of the blade. "I know you've seen this," he said, pulling the sword off the rack.

Divine Mathematics pointed to a part of the blade about three inches from the hand guard. On that spot was a symbol, etched into the surface of the blade that faced the owner when the sword was held in the ready posture. The symbol was two sets of four vertical lines, side-by-side—Eji Ogbe, which meant many things, but in this case, it meant "compassion."

"This is to remind me of my duty," Divine

Mathematics said, pointing to the symbol. "The warrior's way includes an awareness of when to be compassionate, merciful. But, Mack..." he turned the sword around, "My opponent can't see the symbol when I hold the sword. He can only see the blade. That is as it should be."

"I understand, Teacher."

"Do you?" he paused as if considering just how far he wanted to push this. "You gotta commit to things, Mack. Otherwise you run the risk of not only deluding others, but deluding yourself, too."

Divine Mathematics believed that tact was an impediment to serious training.

Janiah was sure that he could have dwelt on her shortcomings indefinitely, but the mid-morning weekend class was beginning to arrive, and she had places to go.

Tony and James were grinding away at the less glamorous side of detecting and investigating, but there was nothing yet. To make things worse, Janiah got a Fed Ex letter saying that President and Mrs. Nix wanted the honor of her to cater a cocktail reception to celebrate the end of the semester. Saturday at two at the presidential mansion. She had prepared the food and her assistants were on their way to the mansion to set up, but her presence had been required by President Nix.

The president's receptions were the talk of the campus. They were lavish beyond the experience of the rank and file. The trajectory of a career at the institution could be measured at these events. People covertly watched one another, mentally ticking off a list of who was willing to be seen with whom. And who wasn't. Nix used the events as public displays of his feelings about people. A professor could get invited so President Nix could fawn all over them.

Or a professor could get all dolled up only to arrive and learn that they've been summoned so President Nix can pointedly snub them. In that case, the only consolation was that the food was great, thanks to Janiah, and the booze was free.

And President Nix paid her handsomely to make sure she served only her greatest culinary masterpieces. Her menu for this afternoon was: curried potato salad, vegan macaroni and "cheese," tenderly smoked collard greens, maple glazed yams, black-eyed peas, seitan pepper steak and cornbread muffins.

***

She drove her old *Ford Fusion* to the party. Normally, she drove her *Yukon Denali*, the last gift from her parents before her father passed, but her assistants were using it to transport food to the party. In any event, the reception was already in full swing when she got there.

Nix's residence bordered the college but was shielded from the gaze of mere mortals by thick hedges. Inside the yard, a striped tent shielded the bar and food tables. The day was warm and sunny, with a light breeze rustling the higher leaves of the big oaks that bordered the property. Various clusters of people were spread around the grounds chatting merrily while a quartet of music majors sawed away dutifully at their violins and cellos.

Janiah took a quick look around, getting the lay of the land. President Nix was nowhere in evidence, which was a relief. She spotted Vice President Flanigan in mid-scheme with a cluster of administrators. A few faculty members stared at her briefly, then turned back to the business at hand.

She went to the bar, swigged some beer, and looked

out at the other guests.

Out strode the president, projecting himself as if there was something tremendously fearless in his decision to brave the force of the sun. He was impeccably outfitted in a tuxedo with a cream-colored jacket and black trousers. He'd made the bold fashion statement of wearing a black paisley ascot instead of a tie. Nix began working the crowd, stopping to have brief, authoritative conversations with small knots of administrators. He churned through them with the look of someone diligently pursuing an unpleasant duty.

Nemesio Pena was in tow. He was dressed in a sporty style—a tan summer suit, blue shirt, and maroon patterned tie—but seemed somehow out of his element.

Then Nix's eyes met Janiah's.

"Oh, no," she whispered involuntary. The president changed course and headed right at her.

Nix did not really smile as most people knew it. The best he could manage was a sort of long foxy grin—a baring of teeth that was more frightening than reassuring—and he gave Janiah one of his best "I will eat your young" grins.

He took her hand. "Ms. Mack, Mr. Pena has been telling me what a marvelous job you did for him."

Nemesio had been lurking in the background with that "Sorry I had to finger you for murder, my mistake" look. On cue, he stepped forward to chime in.

"Fantastic, Ms. Mack. Thanks."

"My pleasure," Janiah said, stunned into courtesy. "Hello, Nemesio." Janiah eyed him for a moment to see whether he would squirm. Not a twitch. He and the president seemed in on a little secret that made them both happy.

But joy was fleeting at the top. The president's head jerked around. "Ah, there is my provost. I must have a word. Mr. Pena, Ms. Mack, you will excuse me."

They nodded and made room as the President got under way.

As a parting shot, he added, "I was telling Mr. Pena how glad we were to be of service to him. We look forward to a long friendship. I am sure you will agree, Ms. Mack." He didn't even wait for a reply, but strode across the yard calling for the provost.

Pena steered Janiah to the end of the bar. He reached into his breast pocket and pulled out two envelopes. He looked at the identifying marks on them, put one back, and handed her what turned out to be the long-awaited check. It was for the amount they had agreed on. Was it rude to peek? Janiah's landlord wouldn't think so.

"Well, things are looking up," she said. Janiah was sure that the other envelope was for the president. It explained his manic good spirits.

"You bet." Pena said. He took a long, grateful pull from his glass. It told Janiah that he had found a private session with Nix to be somewhat stressful. He gestured to the bartender for another and seemed to brighten at the prospect.

"You would not believe the interest this thing is generating, Ms. Mack."

"So the brochure worked out for you? That was quick."

"Hmm? Oh, well, actually I went a step farther," Pena said. "I'm still creating the glossy piece for the opening. But to get things moving, I put it on the Martial Masters web page, Instagram, Facebook and Twitter."

"Smart move," Janiah said.

"You bet," Pena said. The ice cubes clinked against his teeth as he drained the glass. "You've got to keep a high profile on social media, Ms. Mack. Otherwise, the competition will eat you alive."

"And what is the competition doing these days, Nemesio?"

He gave Janiah a broad smile, one that told her he was feeling a bit more himself away from the president. "The competition is eating their hearts out, Ms. Mack. You know, I was worried. What with the murder, I was afraid that the whole show would fall apart. With the setup costs, it could have been a disaster."

Then his predatory optimism just ate right through that rare moment of doubt.

"But let me tell you," he broke into a grin as his vodka was reloaded, "the news coverage has just revved up interest even more. The phone's ringing off the hook. The web page is getting, oh, I don't know, like ten thousand hits a day and I have over eighty thousand followers on Instagram now. All in all, things couldn't have worked out better."

"Except for Mejia," Janiah said. "What with him dyig and all."

Pena looked momentarily chastened again, but it was an emotion that struggled futilely with the selective conscience of the businessman. It took a lot to keep Pena down for long.

"Want to see your stuff? C'mon, we'll use Peter's computer." He drained his third drink and they headed toward the house.

The transition from the sunny yard to the dim quiet of President Nix's study was a bit hard on the eyes, and for a moment Janiah stood there waiting for them to adjust. Nix's home office was something of a disappointment. She knew expected his coffin, maybe some blood-drained victims, but it was really just a tastefully appointed study. Real wood paneling. Abstract artwork. The noise of their footsteps was swallowed up by a plush Persian rug.

Pena booted up the computer. Janiah noticed the machine had a university property tag stuck to the side of it. She wondered whether the art did, too. Pena tapped merrily on the keys for a minute and wiggled the mouse.

The website popped up and they were off on a guided tour of Pena's little cyber-kingdom.

"Okay, here we go." It was a pretty nice graphic image of a waterfall, much like the one in the museum. He clicked on "Legacies of the Masters" to show her the text and pictures of what would eventually be the exhibit catalogue. Sure enough, there was her stuff.

Something on the screen caught her eye: "Modern Masters."

"Hit that," she asked him, touching the screen.

A graphic appeared. It was a shoji—one of those sliding paper doors the Japanese use in traditional homes. Pena clicked on it and it slid to one side, revealing a shot of the dojo at the Martial Masters museum. Superimposed over the picture was the word "masters." He clicked again.

A video clip of Fred Mejia in action appeared.

There was no mistaking the power of the man. It took about two seconds for Mejia to charge the screen with a slashing sword attack, then the image froze and a laudatory summary of Mejia's achievements and expertise appeared.

It didn't mention the fact that he was dead.

"What's this?" Janiah asked.

Nemesio tried to act surprised. "Oh. I guess we need to update that." He reached over for the mouse. They popped back to the home screen. A little message at the bottom informed them we were the 75,486th person to visit the site.

"See what I mean?" he asked. "The news was great publicity. Oh, man." He almost kissed the monitor. "I love it."

"I don't suppose it hurts to have Mejia dancing around there so every reader of the *Daily News* can get a chance to see him, huh Nemesio?" Janiah never really knew Mejia, but flogging his image to drive sales was a bit much.

Pena's grin faded. "Hey, that was on for weeks before the... incident. Besides, I have it rigged so there's a new master every month or so, and there are links to their dojo, dojang, or kwoon and more free publicity than they ever imagined. Don't get all cranky on me, Ms. Mack. Everyone makes out."

He gave her a hard look. "Including you." Nemesio was usually smooth, but she had heard he would cut a competitor's throat in a minute. Seeing that look, she could believe it.

He was right, of course—the check she had in her

pocket was Martial Masters money. But it did not make her feel better. Pena picked up on the sudden coolness in the room. He looked at his watch.

"Ah, God! I better get back out to Peter. Got a little donation ceremony to do." He patted his breast meaningfully. "See you, Ms. Mack." The tone told her that it would be quite some time.

CHAPTER EIGHT

The Mack clan sprung from a very shallow gene pool: they all looked pretty much the same—tall, athletically built, with medium brown skin and strong, handsome or pretty features. When Janiah pulled up in front of Tony's house in the West End, a row of almost indistinguishable children's heads popped up from behind the palisade fence. "Hi Aunt Janiah!" they shrieked, collapsing back down out of sight, giggling.

"Hey, li'l nuggets," Janiah called.

Anthony, one of Tony's children and the birthday boy of the moment, came charging out and grabbed her by the leg.

"Where's my toy? Where's my toy?" He demanded.

"Toy? What toy?" Janiah said. Then, feigning surprise, "Who are you, little boy?" He stopped tugging at her long enough to look confused for a second.

"Aunt Janiah!" He shouted. "You know who I am!" Anthony was almost sure of it, but children are well aware that adults are strange and unpredictable. Almost anything was possible.

Tony's wife, Aisha, had spotted the open gate and came scooting out to drive Anthony back into the corral. "Ant!" she said in that tone mothers everywhere use. "Behave."

Janiah laughed. "Okay, Ant. The loot's in the car," she said. He seemed briefly relieved that she hadn't lost her mind, then went scampering off to get his gift.

"Hi, Aisha," Janiah said.

Aisha had a heart-shaped face with a look almost identical to the actress and singer Keke Palmer, which made sense because she and Keke were first cousins. She smiled, which made her eyes narrow into slits. "Hey girl," she said. "The riot is being held in the back."

As an in-law, Aisha had a somewhat more objective view of the family than Janiah did. She had also benefited from a decade of experience with them. Aisha was nice but usually got right to the point. Life with Tony was not an adventure in subtlety.

Anthony lumbered by with a wrapped box almost as big as he was. Aisha and Janiah followed and closed the gate.

It was early in the season, but Tony had taken the bold step of opening the pool for the children. Atlanta is like Singapore in the summer—hot and humid—but with way more Black folks. A succession of above ground backyard pools had punctuated the vacation months of their childhood, and Tony had replicated that experience for his children.

There were at least twelve bodies flailing around in the water. Janiah knew there were dred-headed, afroed, and even permed Mack family members in there, but soaking wet, they all looked alike. Occasionally, one would emerge for a toweling down, trembling with cold, and then leap back in for a screaming, splashing dance with hypothermia. A few Mack children only came out to eat.

Most of the men were by the barbecue. Janiah's two other brothers, Jermaine and Trent, were there. So was James. Janiah spotted his wife, Fatou, over by the sliding glass door that led to the kitchen and gave her a wave. Janiah's sister Desiree was doing lifeguard duty by the pool. Her other sister, Kendra, was probably in the kitchen, deep in recipes concocted with huge helpings of *Louisiana Hot Sauce.*

Janiah's brothers-in-law were two pleasant men who, as time went on, began to get looks on their faces that said life with her sisters was more than they had bargained for. Between the two of them, they had nine children under the age of ten. They enjoyed the barbecues—they got to talk to adults, tell off-color jokes they had been hoarding for weeks, and furtively drink more beer than permitted. Both men were starting to lose their hair.

There was music and stories, various minor accidents with the children, and the normal type of socializing that goes on with a group of people who know each other very well, and generally get along well despite the fact. In short, the rest of the afternoon passed in the subdued riot that passes for get-togethers with family.

After cake and presents, as evening came on, Janiah sat on a molded plastic lawn chair, a little apart from the crush of the family. She could still smell the charcoal in the air. One of the neighbors had a baseball game on the TV and the faint roar of the stadium crowd could be heard. A few of the smaller children rolled around in discarded wrapping paper away from the presents.

This was pretty much the way it was for Janiah growing up. When she thought about it, she mostly remembered crowds—children and adults—Christmases, birthdays, and barbecues. She jerked her legs out of the way as one of Kendra's children shot by, trying to catch a lightning bug. She had memories of similar hunts, running with small tribes of children on broad expanses of freshly cut lawns—a breathless pursuit in the moist blueness of a summer night.

Her mother was in Chicago visiting her sister. Otherwise, they would probably be at her house destroying her lawn. Her father, the king of barbecues, had died of cancer nearly two years ago. He had given it a good fight. But at the end, there wasn't much left of him. *Fuck cancer*, she thought.

Janiah smiled and looked around the backyard. At times like this, she recalled her father the way he was. She could almost hear him in the crowd. It's one of the reasons she kept coming to family parties, she supposed.

Tony had been shooting her looks all day, squinting significantly through the smoke of barbecue and birthday cake candles. With everyone fed and presents unwrapped, it was time to rendezvous in the family room. James slipped in after her, pulling the sliding glass doors to the yard closed.

The family room looked like the place old overstuffed furniture went to die.

"What's up, Tony?" Janiah whispered.

"James' been following up with that detective Gregoire from New Orleans," James said. "He's getting details to see whether there's some sort of connection between the two murders."

Janiah turned to James. "And?"

"You, my sister, are looking at the Sherlock Holmes of cyberspace," he commented with a big smile.

"The Pink Panther, maybe," Tony said under his breath.

James shot him a look and went on. "It turns out that there have been at least two other homicides of this type in the last week."

"Come on!" Janiah protested. "The papers would have a field day."

"Straight up, " James said. "But the murders didn't take place in the same area. Homicide is local crime, and these things happened in different states. Unless you're looking, you wouldn't find 'em."

"The killer's method is slightly different each time," Tony chimed in.

James shrugged. "Basic underlying pattern is the same," he said.

"What pattern?" I asked.

"The other two victims were also prominent martial arts instructors." James said, ticking the point off on his finger. "The victims checked out clean. No problems with gangs, drugs or domestic violence. No disgruntled students."

"No disgruntled lovers," Tony added.

"Both were male and both were killed in somewhat exotic ways."

Janiah raised an eyebrow and James answered the

unasked question, "Dude in New Orleans was stabbed to death with a broken stick. A couple of days later, a Brazilian national in Austin, Texas named Coutinho went down."

"Jair Coutinho?" Janiah asked, shocked.

"You knew him?" James asked.

Janiah nodded. Jair Coutinho was the real thing. He was a champion in Brazilian Jujitsu who had capped a successful tournament career in Brazil by relocating to the U.S. to promote the sport here. Janiah had never met him, but he was said to be charming and talented. Coutinho was, from all reports, a master technician, a skilled teacher, and had a real flair for self-promotion. The Brazilians loved him. They called him Guerreiro Bonito—"Pretty Warrior," and when he left Bahia, his fans wailed.

Janiah could not believe that Divine Mathematics had not mentioned it. She couldn't believe Guerreiro Bonito was dead.

"He sustained a number of serious injuries from some sort of weapon," James said. "But the actual cause of death was strangulation."

"No rope," Tony said. "Bruises are consistent with a fairly sophisticated choking technique."

"Okay, pretty gruesome," Janiah said, still trying to adjust to the surprise. "But how is it unusual?"

"Most homicides are fairly routine in turns of motive," Tony said. "You got guns, knives, and blunt instruments."

"With beatings, you usually get a victim who has been worked over," James said. "*All* over. Death is usually from internal bleeding and it takes a while. Now for stranglings, you got your ropes, wires, and what have you. Ligature strangulation and manual. Crime of passion, lots of thumb marks on the front. These kinds of killers like their victims to see them."

"But what we see here is different," Tony said.

"How so?" Janiah asked.

"Whoever did this was a pro," James said. "The victims in both New Orleans and Austin were not subject to wild, unfocused beatings; which is what you usually get. Rage killings. In these cases, someone pounded the shit out of them, but man, he knew where to pound. The choke job was the same type of thing. Focused."

"You know, it's hard work beating someone to death," Tony said. "Most times, it takes a while. Usually, some restraints are involved. But not here. These killings were almost surgical. The bruises tell us that a pro did it."

"Let me ask you a question," Janiah said. "You're always talking about bruises on the victims. It seems to me that it takes a while for a bruise to form. I know you get some discoloration on a body after death—"

"Postmortem lividity," James said.

"Right. But that has to do with blood settling. How do you get bruises like the ones you're talking about? If the victim is killed relatively quickly after the injury?"

James' eyebrows shot up. "Pretty smart, Janiah," he said. He looked at Tony. "Are you sure you two are related?"

Tony grinned. He gestured for James and Janiah to wait. The glass door slid back and let some of the party noise wash into the room. He came back in with some beers from the big orange cooler on the patio and shook the ice chips off as he handed them to his friend and sister. Then he walled the family off again and continued.

"When you first look at the corpse, you don't see the bruises," Tony told her. "Then you have the M.E. stick him in the cooler overnight." He popped the tab on the can and took a drink.

"Then you see the bruises," James said. "Sort of like developing a picture."

"Okay, I got it," Janiah said.

"To get back to the issue here," James said, "both the other victims appear to have been killed somewhere in the early part of the morning. And—"

"And," Tony chimed in.

"Someone signed '1488' at each scene."

Janiah sat back in her chair. "Oh, no."

"Oh, yes," James said. "The messages are slightly different, though."

"How so?" she asked.

"The New Orleans murder just had the signature '1488,'" James replied.

"In Austin, the killer added: 'I'm coming.' Then the same signature," James said.

"So what does that tell you?" Janiah asked.

"Details of the 1488 thing were not released to the press in the Wulff murder. So a copycat is out of the picture," James said. "The killings are geographically dispersed, but they follow a pattern."

"We got a request in for a DNA sample from the New Orleans killing," James told me. "We'll compare it with samples from the Coutinho and Mejia murders. It'll take a few days, but we'll see if they match up."

"You know they'll match up, James," Tony said.

"Okay... and if they match up, what does that mean?" Janiah asked.

"It means that we have a nut job on the loose that gets off starring in his own Jackie Chan snuff films," James said.

"Well, does it narrow things down for you in terms of suspects?" Janiah asked. "You know, give you a handle on what the killer might look like?"

"We know he's probably a male," James said. "But that's not a big help. Statistically, most murderers are. He's about five feet nine or ten inches tall and probably right handed."

"Gee, Sherlock, did you figure all that out by yourself?" Tony asked. Then he looked at Janiah and smirked. "Don't be too impressed, sis." He gazed at his friend. "I read the site analysis from the crime lab, too, J."

James looked sheepish.

"They do an analysis of this kind of thing," James explained. "You'd be amazed. From splatter marks, position of the body—"

"Star signs, phases of the moon, mood rings." Tony added. "They can come up with a profile of the killer—his probable sex, age, size. It's weird."

"It's police science," James said. "It works. These forensic guys know their shit."

"But other than that, the police don't have much," Tony said. "The DNA comparison is only gonna help them when they get a suspect in custody."

Tony squinted off into the distant yard, thinking. "Right now, Janiah, the assumption is that this guy is white because of the 1488 stuff. Probably from up North. Whoever it is has been pretty well trained and he's brutal. It's the same in both cases. He's into this martial arts shit as his method. You look at the victims; they're connected by the arts. And killed by them."

James held up his empty beer can and looked at it as if he suspected evaporation as the culprit. Tony got us another round.

"On the one hand, he might be Asian—Japanese, more likely," James said. "The Japanese don't have much love for Black folks, either, and love white folks, so he might believe in the 1488 ideology. If he *is* some Japanese national visiting the area, we should have INS records."

"Summer in the city," Tony said. "I'll bet there are thousands of Japanese tourists in town."

"Nah, more like thirty or forty," James said. "There are only 4,254 Japanese in Atlanta Metro. Cobb, DeKalb and Fulton are home to 62 percent of the Japanese in Metro and 39 percent of the Japanese living in the whole state, so we've got it narrowed down a bit."

"How're you gonna run him down?" Janiah asked. "Most Japanese visitors will be traveling in groups—with their families or other tourists. This guy probably won't."

"Ya see?" Tony said. "It gets better and better. We've

got it narrowed down even more." He paused and looked at James. They didn't say anything, but Janiah got the sense of messages flying back and forth through the air. Messages she was not meant to hear.

James sat forward in his chair and began to speak very slowly and clearly to Janiah. "So think about this, Janiah. The link is through Japan—even if the person of interest is white, he's spent ample time there training—and the martial arts."

She said nothing, just sipped some beer and watched him work. "So there are three prominent martial artists," he continued.

"And this guy is... I dunno, tracking them down."

"You sure?" Janiah asked him.

"Oh yeah," James said. "The sequence is too tight." He ticked the points off one by one. "New Orleans... Austin... now here. All within days of one another. The killer is traveling. Messages seem to pretty much bear that interpretation out: all that 'I am coming, I am here' shit."

"Dramatic as hell," Tony said with a nod.

But something was bothering Janiah. "You know, I don't see Mejia as being in the same class as Wulff and Coutinho. Not at all."

James nodded. "There's a link between victims we don't see yet. Mejia was Mexican and Cuban and raised in Atlanta; Wulff was German and lived in New Orleans; Coutinho was from Salvador, Bahia, Brazil."

"Mejia practiced Kuk Sool Won," Janiah added. "Wulff practiced Wing Chun and Coutinho practiced Brazilian Jujitsu. Totally different arts."

"You follow a trail, it's because it leads to something," Tony said quietly. "The trail leads here. The writing confirms it. In New Orleans, it was just the signature, a kind of general announcement. Then Austin, a type of warning. But here, the message is that he's arrived."

"Question is, who's supposed to be getting the message?" James said.

"There's something we don't know about what's happening right under our noses," Tony said. "Someone local is reading that message and knowing what it means."

"What!" Janiah could not believe it.

The expression on their faces told her they were disappointed. So her brother filled her in.

"There's something your pal Holy Calculus ain't tellin' us."

"You know his name," Janiah said. "Divine Mathematics. And come on, this is all speculation. You don't really know anything for sure."

"It feels right to me," Tony said flatly. He looked questioningly at James.

"My gut says 'yeah', too," James replied.

They waited for Janiah to say something.

"Maybe whoever is doing this is just a nut," Janiah protested. "The victims might not be linked."

"Then why kill them?" her brother asked.

"I know something about Wulff," Janiah said. "He was a pretty prominent Wing Chun instructor. Real old school. Very well respected. Coutinho was, too. I can dig around and see what I can find out. But they're both celebrities of a type."

"Celebrities?" Tony sounded incredulous.

"Well, in the martial arts world," she said with a shrug.

"Janiah, are you saying that Wulff and Coutinho got whacked because 1488 thought they were famous?" James said. "I dunno. We'll keep it in mind, but what about Mejia?"

Janiah shrugged.

"I still think there's a connection," Tony finished.

Janiah shrugged again.

"But think of the fun we could have," James said with glee. "A celebrity."

"Killed by a stalker. " Tony had that look in his eye.

James continued. "A *celebrity* stalker."

"Don't do this, " Janiah pleaded. But it was too late.

Tony went on. "A *samurai* celebrity stalker."

James pointed triumphantly to the ceiling. "A *psycho* samurai celebrity stalker."

Which seemed to sum it all up nicely.

Thye sat for a while longer, drinking more beer. As Janiah went outside, Tony was punching numbers into the phone, working the angles.

"Janiah," he called, and she turned back into the room.

"Yeah, Tony?"

"Something like this… we know what we're doin'," he said. "Trust me. Talk to Divine Mathematics for us."

Janiah nodded but did not feel too good about it.

CHAPTER NINE

At the heart of both sound and movement there is vibration. Divine Mathematics wanted his students to be sensitive to sound. According to the teacher, different types of activity, different places, had distinct aural signatures. Sound laid bare the essence of an activity, its spirit. Remaining open to the message that sound sent could help the warrior in combat and in life, in general.

Janiah had sensed the sounds of the approaching end of the semester all week, even as she grew increasingly distracted by the murder. When she closed her eyes to rest them from the strain of writing end of the semester evaluations of her assistants and checking her invoices, Janiah saw the stark finality of Mejia, collapsed and cold at the crime scene. And on the wall, the message that he was there, with the signature of 1488. The number indicated a white person was the killer, but his skill level and focus said he was Asian. But it was possible for a white man to train in Asian martial arts to the same level as the best Asian martial artists—Steven Seagal had and had even taught in Japan; Chuck Norris had; Richard Norton; Bas Rutten.

Janiah's brother was waiting for a DNA report, but it

didn't slow him down. While Janiah was still thinking about killers and exotic martial arts techniques, Tony got right down to the nitty gritty of investigating.

"It's not like the movies," he preached to Janiah. "Whoever this killer is, he needs to eat; he needs a place to sleep." Tony believed grunt work would eventually lead them to the killer. But there was the sense of the ticking of a clock, of time slipping away, because 1488 was out there.

Tony had taken a quick look at things from Janiah's end, trying to get some information on the two victims—anything that might give them a clue to 1488's identity and how he chose his victims.

One would think that the world of martial arts would be a small place, but once you started looking, you found all sorts of organizations, causes, and publications. The mainstream popular martial arts world was pretty well-covered by periodicals and their websites, like *Black Belt*, *Inside Kung-Fu* and *Karate/Kung Fu Illustrated*, but there was a host of others that sprang up overnight and faded away almost as quickly. Janiah found a library that kept back copies of the most well established and used them as a starting point.

Of course, the library collection was not complete—the martial arts reading public was poor but enthusiastic and tended to steal back issues with shocking regularity. Janiah was able to plug some of the holes by consulting the back lists that got included with every month's issue and searching on the internet. Janiah used a contact at the library to request copies of missing back articles she felt might be useful. Like her brother, Janiah would have to wait on some things, but she plowed ahead.

It was a fairly tedious process. She sat at a series of battered wooden tables, leafing through back issues that were limp and slightly aromatic with age. She spent hours on Google and websites for relevant articles. Most of the information was slowly coming together.

Wulff was a fairly prominent Wing Chun sifu. His name had been vaguely familiar to Janiah even at the onset. There was coverage of him on and off over the years in magazines and online news sites. He had made a big splash when he first came to this country in the '80s. He had a tremendous pedigree: a gifted fighter and teacher who at one time been asked to help train Grenzschutzgruppe 9—Border Protection Group 9 of the German Federal Police—the elite tactical unit of the German Federal Police. In short order, he became a well-established instructor in New Orleans. He was a big proponent of weapons training in Wing Chun. Traditional Wing Chun only used two weapons—the Bat Jam Do, or short double Butterfly Swords and the Luk Dim Boon Quan, or Dragon Pole. We already knew that a jagged piece of a training staff had been used to kill him. In the weeks before the killing, Wulff was in the news for helping out with choreography and technical advice for a new movie. It was the third installment of *Filthy Bastard*, an action film in which the wisecracking star is eventually stripped down to just his jeans and boots and he takes a volume of punishment that would rival the three-day torture scene in *The Passion of the Christ* before killing the villain and his horde of henchmen. When it hit theaters, fans would be able to glimpse Wulff as an extra in one of the fight scenes.

But there was more to him than that. For all his success, Wulff was a sifu that never lost sight of the real purpose of training. He was quoted in one article as insisting that the true pursuit of Wing Chun was not in perfecting fighting technique but in the spiritual development of what Wulff referred to as "Nei Gong"—the focus on building up chi in the lower belly, the body's energy center, and then using the mind to manipulate, lead, and use that chi for efficient, effective physical manifestations. From the various things Janiah read about Wulff, she got the sense that he was both tremendously skilled and very balanced in his approach to the martial arts.

Coutinho, the Austin victim, was already known to Janiah by reputation. He had been in the United States for only a few months before he was killed. He had been part of a concerted effort to get Brazilian Jujitsu accepted as an Olympic Sport and had launched a series of ambitious seminars that attracted a nationwide audience. Coutinho possessed impressive charisma—they didn't call him the Beautiful Warrior for nothing.

The two dead men had been prominent and skilled martial artists, but other than that, Janiah got no sense of how they were connected. And Mejia's connection was still unknown, which brought her to a dead end. So Janiah considered 1488. Tony looked at the basics. Janiah followed his line of thinking from her own perspective. She thought that someone like 1488 needed not only a place to live, but also a place to train. You didn't acquire and maintain the level of skill that 1488 had without consistent intense training, which is why so many people began studying the martial arts but so few persevered long enough to really learn anything. In a consumer society, where everything is fast and easy, learning the martial arts is not a hot commodity.

Janiah explained to Tony and James that training would probably eat up a big part of 1488's day and be expensive. It narrowed things down somewhat: they had a much better chance of trying to find him by locating likely places where he would and could train.

At his skill level, some training took place alone—running, stretching, lifting weights. However, if someone was serious about combat, then they eventually had to spar. They needed bodies to work with, to hit, to hit them back, to move around and to throw.

For 1488, the kind of place he would need would be special. It would need to be tough. And mean. The type of place Atlanta had in abundance. But he seemed to gravitate to the Japanese arts. Janiah would look for him in a dojo but not some store-front school that was part day care and part hipster fantasy. The people in it would have to be very skilled, which cut down the number of places considerably. Janiah also thought, given the type of things that he would be training in, that there would have to be a high tolerance for injury. When this man practiced, there would be a good likelihood of collateral damage. It narrowed the list down even more.

She had some ideas, but it was a bit out of her league, forcing her to do the one thing that she wanted to avoid. Janiah needed to talk with Divine Mathematics.

Janiah used the excuse that she needed to know about likely places to look for 1488.

Divine Mathematics didn't give her much. Janiah spoke to him during a pause in a training session, so maybe he was focused on something else, but his whole manner seemed odd. Janiah sidled in through the door and saluted, removing her shoes. Janiah waited for the lesson to close and then approached him.

Generally speaking, Divine Mathematics strides the practice floor in isolation. Even when not teaching, people watch him covertly. The way he moves, even the way he breathes can show you something. It was unusual that he should be approached and even more unusual that Janiah did so in street clothes. But she apologized for the intrusion, explained herself quietly to him and hoped he would have a suggestion that could help.

He didn't look at her when he answered the question. And he was pretty vague for the most part. Not particularly helpful. Janiah had given up trying to anticipate his moods and figured that in his brain he was seated in an empty space, staring into nothingness or some other deep shit. But Janiah was mildly surprised by the fact that, after she pushed him for a little more information, he began to appear almost visibly agitated by the whole thing. That was unusual for a man devoted to always appearing cool. It wasn't that Divine Mathematics was not passionate. It was just that permitting others to see his passion gave potential opponents an advantage.

Janiah mentioned Wulff's name and saw no reaction in her teacher's eyes. He had heard something about the man's death, he admitted, but he was unaware of any connection between that incident and Coutinho's murder. When Janiah explained the theory Tony was working on, he dismissed it with a wave of his hand.

"This country has gone to hell in a hand basket," he said. "All those gangster raps and caper shows and horror movies and reality shows. Coutinho's murder... Janiah, I hope your brother don't waste his time chasing illusions. There ain't no mystery here; only tragedy."

But Janiah insisted that Mejia's death proved that 1488 was now in Atlanta and that he was a martial artist. If so, she wanted to help find him. "And that's why your insight would be helpful," she told her teacher. In the end, she got little concrete information from him, despite her finagling. She only got a warning.

"This man you seek, Mack—" Divine Mathematics

stared off blankly at the wall for a moment, then finally turned his hard eyes on her and started again. "Human beings are conduits of power. Training focuses that power; directs it. Men like the one you seek... they're like... they're like electrical cables with holes in 'em. They leak power... and they're dangerous. Their power is the result of a flaw, not of real strength."

He stood, then stutter stepped forward and side to side rhythmically as he brushed his shoulders with his fingertips and lightly tapped the sides of his forehead. An onlooker might think he was dancing, but Janiah knew that he was building up his ase—his vital force; what Asian stylists called chi or ki. *Showing me what real strength is.* "They leak power because of flaws in themselves," he said. "Flaws in their training. They appear impressive. Some people are seduced by them. But their energy is wrong. They're wrong... broken. I wish you would avoid them."

"I'm not looking for a fight, Teacher," Janiah said. "We're just trying to track this killer down."

Divine Mathematics shifted slightly on his feet. "It don't matter what you wish. You're placing yourself in danger."

Janiah was curious. "Are you saying that I wouldn't be able to beat somebody like this killer?"

His eyes narrowed. "Don't be a doggone fool, Mack. It's childish to ask who would win, who would lose. This man—whoever he is—is a murderer."

Divine Mathematics put a firm hand on her shoulder. "Evil's got its own spirit, Mack. Getting too close to it allows it to affect yours. It's crazier than a mug to mess with it."

And he would not say anything more than that.

Tony and James planned to visit different martial arts schools where 1488 might train. Janiah could imagine it. They would slog through a number of dingy gyms, schools with mats stained with blood and sweat and decades-old heavy bags patched with duct tape. They would go into dungeon-like basements and into spaces where the bricks had been painted with diluted whitewash some time during the Vietnam War. The clank of free weights hitting the ground would compete with the staccato rhythm of speed bags and the deeper thuds of bodies hitting the mat in a roped in area farther back in a cavernous space.

The men training there would be mostly young and thickly built. There was no Spandex worn in those training halls, just crisp uniforms with black belts so worn they were nearly falling to pieces and lots of tape on hands and feet. Some of the students and teachers would take one look at Tony and James and duck away, feigning a renewed interest in training.

In those places, the air reeked of strain, frustration, the quest for dominance and anger. The din of thuds and clanks would fill the dimly lit rooms.

Tony and James would ask whether anyone new had been training. They would be greeted with blank looks or faked attempts at thinking. They would go through the motions, leaving their cards and asking if anyone remembered anything or saw anything to give them a call.

They would leave the more exotic locations to her, figuring Janiah would have better luck. Janiah knew some guys in some of the tougher martial arts schools in Atlanta. She was not exactly friends with them, but she had gotten to know them over the years, and even spar with a few.

***

Janiah had first come across Franklin "Freight Train" Davis when she was in college. He was a former wrestler who had taken a shine to judo and was working out on the mats that got shared with the other martial arts clubs. He had gotten hooked on judo and eventually began studying Yoshinkan aikido as well—an art form that added joint locks to the throws and balance shifts of his judo. Aikido in general was a beautiful art and, in highly trained hands, could be somewhat effective. Yoshinkan was a bit on the hard side, using more power than other styles, so it suited Freight Train and was a good supplement to Judo.

The Japanese sensei liked to keep their students on a tight leash: they didn't mind fighting; they just wanted to be able to control when and where their students did it. Freight Train liked fighting so much he kept his teachers worried. From what Janiah knew of him and the type of people who gravitated to his dojo, Janiah thought he might be able to point her in a good direction.

Like many other Atlanta martial arts schools, Freight Train's had to offer classes practically around the clock to survive. It was especially hard since he was a Black man. Black men that taught anything other than Tae Kwon Do aimed at children had it hard. Except for Divine Mathematics, who taught African martial arts, so he had a niche.

Freight Train taught an early morning workout for stressed corporate types. He had typical evening classes and even an early lunchtime session on Sundays, which was where Janiah found Freight Train putting his pupils through their paces.

He was a man of average size, but with muscles hard as granite and anyone who ever tangled with Freight Train learned that he was freakishly strong. He had a big, square head with short, fuzzy black hair and a neck like a section of an old tree trunk. There were nicks in his skull, scars from old fights where the hair would never grow back. Freight Train took his training seriously. His eyes were nearly black and his skin was just as dark. He had that focused stare you see with really intense competitors that was designed to frighten their opponents. His face was lean, and you could see that the straight ridge of his nose had been ruined when it was broken.

Janiah did not know if he was still mad at her for doing it years ago when students from Black Fists and Afros would meet up with students from other schools and spar… until Divine Mathematics found out. Janiah figured they were even, though: she could not sleep on her right side because of something he did to her shoulder.

The dojo was a pretty good size, located in an old downtown warehouse. The walls and pipes had been painted over and over again in white to make you believe that things were new and clean. It mostly looked dingy and tired.

But the mats in Freight Train's school were in good shape. They were worn but repaired precisely. He had about twenty men, all at black belt level, working on some take down techniques. In Yoshinkan aikido, they tend to just wear a judo gi and not the fancier pleated hakama skirts other aikido black belts wear. It sends a certain message about the tough, no frills approach the style takes to fighting.

Freight Train was working with the class on deflecting a lunging punch and then throwing the attacker by unbalancing him and moving in with a forearm strike across his neck. Freight Train spotted Janiah's entrance out of the corner of his eye. His glanced her way, but he made no sign of recognition.

Janiah had seen the technique before, in Steven Seagal movies. It was the main technique he did throughout *Above the Law*, putting down the bad guys hard and making aikido look cool. But the way Freight Train taught it was gritty and vicious. *Still smooth and cool, though*, she thought.

Freight Train's demonstrated several times and then the class got to try. He watched as they paired off and tried out his variations on each other.

Janiah watched with him. And listened.

The sounds here were serious—the rhythmic slam of bodies hitting the mat; the deep thud of bodies colliding; the hiss of breath; the occasional grunt. Janiah also picked up the high-pitched sound of slapping.

Freight Train sidled up to her. "Janiah. You come for a workout?" It wasn't a friendly comment. Freight Train and men like him worked hard at things, making them good at what they did, but they also tended to believe that their way was the only way.

"No," Janiah said, shaking his hand. "I'm just looking for some help with something."

The slapping sound continued, drawing her attention.

Freight Train saw her glance and gestured with his chin. "Check this guy out. He's the real deal."

The man wore a pristine white gi that looked soft from repeated washings. He was intent on working his partner relentlessly, moving in repeatedly to practice the move that Freight Train had shown them. The slapping noise was from his cupped hand sharply slamming into the jaw of his partner as a prelude to the throw. In his partner's brief moment of pain, the man would whirl into position and then execute the throw. His victim would be driven to the mat and then rise, red-faced from the blow, to take more.

Freight Train did not look concerned as he watched. He did not say anything. It was a tough place.

Janiah told him about her problem. He looked at his class for a minute as if inspecting a lineup of suspects. "My people are tough, Janiah, but I don't see any of them as a murderer."

"Sure, Freight Train," Janiah said. "But if anyone new comes by, anyone out of the ordinary, please, let me know."

He gave her a hard stare. "I run a business here, Janiah," he said. "People come in to train. I got transients coming by all the time. What's it gonna do for me if I start getting them involved with the cops? It'll kill me."

"Funny you should say that. The guy I'm looking for kills people."

He shook his head. "I teach people to fight. I don't get involved with their lives off the mat."

Janiah could see he was annoyed. Freight Train always had a short fuse. Janiah changed the subject and nodded in his student's direction. "He's going at it a bit hard, isn't he? Is he always this intense?" Part of her was wondering if the intense man fit the profile of the one that the police were looking for.

Freight Train crossed his arms across his chest and

watched the class. "Pretty much." Then he looked at Janiah. "Don't get any ideas. He's been with me for a few years."

Janiah felt let down. She figured that she was not going to crack the case. Freight Train watched as the man's partner took a particularly hard fall. Janiah winced, but Freight Train was stoic.

"Ya gotta keep him away from the beginners," Freight Train said. "They tend to break. He gives my advanced people a run for their money, though. Hang on a sec."

He glided over to the mat's edge—as hard and crude as he was, he practically floated—then called the group to order. He told everyone to take a short break and called the intense man over.

The Real Deal was cautiously polite in a way that's typical of many martial artists. They save most of their intensity for training. "Sensei Davis tells us stories about your school," he said. "And your teacher. It would be something to meet him."

"Get in line," Freight Train said. "But don't get your hopes up. I've been trying to get in there and train for years. Add some of that striking they've got to my arsenal." The topic seemed to revive his bad mood. "What he sees in you is anybody's guess, Janiah."

Janiah just shrugged. She sometimes wondered the same thing. But she knew that Freight Train would not be getting to see Divine Mathematics any time soon. Her teacher had spoken to her about Freight Train in the past. He wanted the hotheaded sensei to get more control of his emotions and arrogance before Divine Mathematics let him in.

Freight Train smirked at her. "Okay, since you're here, how about a quick lesson for the class?" he said. "Show us some of those African and street techniques you work on."

Both men looked at her expectantly. If they were not going to get to see Divine Mathematics anytime soon, maybe some pointers from one of his students would do. But that was not the only reason. Way back in the eyes of the two men, Janiah could see the predatory gleam of competitors. They wanted to see her work.

Freight Train ushered the class back into order and introduced her. Janiah slipped her shoes off and saluted before stepping onto the mat.

She gestured for a partner. The student that had been working with the "Real Deal" stepped forward. Half of his face was still red from the slapping he had gotten. Janiah gave the man credit for guts.

She looked around the group. "In the African martial arts we say, 'ti o ba ti wa nibẹ, lo o'—'if it's there, use it'," Janiah began. "Or as y'all say in judo, 'maximum efficiency for a minimum of effort'."

Some heads nodded around the circle that had formed around her. "In a fight, you might try a technique and it doesn't quite work—the temptation is very strong to compensate by overpowering the opponent." Janiah turned to her partner, gesturing at him, "Come at me; full-speed, please."

He came at her with a strong front punch-reverse punch combination. "Somebody centered," Janiah said as she side-stepped, "somebody strong and well-trained, like this guy here, is hard to fight off." The man's punches missed. He attacked again, this time striking with a reverse punch, followed by a back-fist as he stepped forward, then another reverse punch with his other hand.

Janiah blocked the first punch with the horizontal elbow of the 52 Blocks Skull and Bones technique. She then used Open Door to stuff the power of his back-fist and finally slammed a hammer-fist downward onto his arm as he launched his second reverse punch.

The man staggered backward, rubbing his aching forearm.

"Being too timid, or too slow, sets you up for defeat. Ogun—the Spirit of War—blesses the bold and the swift."

Janiah nodded at the man and he assumed a cat-like stance, preparing to attack again. "In your school, being too timid is not an issue," Janiah said. "But being too slow is. This is not an insult, it is a fact. Your stance is the problem—there is no rhythmic movement. If you know physics, an object at rest tends to stay at rest."

The man attacked harder, faster, trying to prove that the Japanese arts were not slow.

"This is where the temptation to use too much strength has come in," Janiah said, evading and deflecting the man's blows with ease. "It's a natural reaction: crank up the volume. You're punching faster with your hands, but your feet are still slow. It is footwork that drives all technique."

The man attacked again without Janiah prompting him. He leapt forward with a hard, thrusting front kick.

Janiah dropped her level as she brought a vertical elbow downward, slamming it into the small bones at the top of the man's foot.

He winced in pain and then his foot dropped to the mat.

Janiah grabbed the man's wrist and the back of his neck, yanked him forward and off-balance, then turned her back to him and slammed the back of her thigh into the front of his, launching him high over her shoulder.

The man's back slammed into the mat with a loud thud. He lay there, gasping for air.

"Footwork telegraphs your attack or conceals it," Janiah said. "Footwork adds power to your technique or weakens it. Footwork drives all technique."

Janiah saluted her partner. Her partner bowed.

The students clapped.

As Janiah walked off the mat, she felt the energy of someone staring at her. She turned to find Freight Train's hard-case student standing near the end of the mat, the wheels turning in his head as he thought about her demonstration.

He probably thinks he can take me, she thought.

Janiah nodded in his direction. Then she got out of there before he got a chance to test his theory.

CHAPTER TEN

Janiah went home that night uneasy. She felt some sort of psychic shift taking place. It was not a good thing. Divine Mathematics called this "apeta"—a type of fear that a powerful martial artist could force on a lesser opponent, without seeming to do anything. Apeta is unseen but nonetheless real. Janiah had a sense of something pushing against her, probing her weaknesses.

If she had to explain it to someone, she did not know if she could. There was a nagging thought just out of reach of her conscious recognition, like a word just on the tip of one's tongue. All Janiah was left with was a feeling that a storm was building.

***

Pena had gone on with his plans for a gala opening of the exhibit at Martial Masters. Even if decency had made him reconsider it—and no one who knew him entertained the thought that he had any decency—the post murder notoriety would have made the allure of publicity far too strong for his lack of ethics to withstand.

He had wanted to kick the night off with a

demonstration of some of the best martial arts the Atlanta area had to offer. In keeping with developments, he had gotten more than he bargained for. Divine Mathematics wanted in.

Martial arts masters like Divine Mathematics tended to keep people like Nemesio Pena at arm's length, but now honor was involved. With a little digging, Janiah found out that the wooden sword that was taken the night of Mejia's murder was not a minor showpiece. It was a training weapon used by Yasuke, a samurai retainer of African origin who served under the Japanese feudal lord Oda Nobunaga from 1579 to 1582. If the local martial arts masters were relatively unmoved by Mejia's murder, they felt the theft of Yasuke's weapon to be a direct affront, Divine Mathematics included. Yasuke was one of two men that inspired Divine Mathematics to begin learning martial arts. The other was his great uncle, Ekene Obiako, a Captain in the elite 72nd Special Forces Battalion of Nigeria, a master of Gidigbo and the Nigerian Army's most decorated soldier.

Divine Mathematics had been to the meeting the masters held with Pena. The senior masters all vowed to help find the thief. In addition, the memories of both Wulff and Coutinho would be honored at the gala. The masters felt that Pena's stable of fake warriors, commandos, and ninja were not up to the task, so they insisted on their inclusion in the events surrounding the display, which is why Janiah was there a day before the big event. Divine Mathematics had sent her to make sure that the arrangements for the demonstration space were adequate. Pena's staff had given assurances, but Divine Mathematics refused to believe it. It was not just his contempt for Pena, it was that, when it came to a public display, Divine Mathematics left nothing to chance.

So Janiah went back to Martial Masters and spoke with the display's curator. The wooden floor of the exhibition gallery was glossy with polish—people would never know that they had shoveled Mejia into a rubber bag in that very space just a week ago. The curator was a narrow-faced woman who sniffed constantly, as if catching a sudden whiff of something unpleasant. She seemed only too happy to let Janiah wander off by herself.

The temporary dividers for the display had been removed, revealing a cavernous space. Behind a vacant performance area, you could glimpse the glass cases and muted lighting of the exhibit. Divine Mathematics had given Janiah precise specifications to check. Even though part of her was consumed with the memory of the museum as a crime scene, Janiah complied with her teacher's wishes. She checked for pillars that were jutting out and walked the floor, checking for irregularities and splinters. The wall where 1488 had commemorated the murder with his message and signature had been repainted. Janiah was alone in the space where 1488 had left his mark.

Janiah paced the perimeter of the space, trying to recreate Mejia's last fight. Janiah could imagine the grunts, the hisses of air, and the contained lunges. *Were they barefoot? Did they speak to each other? What do you say to someone when you realize they're trying to kill you?* Janiah thought. *When he finally looked into the eyes of his killer, what did he see? What does anybody see at that moment?*

In the martial arts, students train to diminish the ego. Janiah had been chipping away at hers for years, but she hoped that the eventual diminishing of self occurred at her own pace and was not thrust upon her in some crazy death match.

The next night, she stood uncomfortably at the

reception with the masters, outfitted in their best ceremonial garb—fancy but still able to demonstrate in. Divine Mathematics wore a navy blue "senator"—a long-sleeved, pullover linen shirt with a rounded collar, with a hem that extended a little past the top of the thighs and matching skinny-leg linen pants. The shirt had a gold stripe around its collar and down the center of its chest. On his feet, the teacher wore blue leather *Fenton Lace-Up* dress sneakers. Divine Mathematics' signature blue flat cap was tilted on his head.

Janiah matched Divine Mathematics in a navy blue dashiki with light blue accents and skinny-leg pants with the same print. She wore the same *Fenton Lace-Up* shoes.

An excited crowd of well-dressed martial arts aficionados and students eagerly waited for something to happen.

The masters, of course, were seething. Standing there, elegant and self-contained, you could not tell, but there was an intensity the masters had in their eyes.

The emotional atmosphere in the room was cluttered. Divine Mathematics wanted Janiah to be more open to those unconscious signals, so she was trying hard to sense things. The vibes she was picking up were not very comforting. People tried to look cool, but their energy was bouncing around like agitated electrons. Only the various masters were still. They regarded the crowds, dispassionate and removed, silent judges from another world. They stood there, mute and hard amid the smoothness of shark skin tuxedos, evening gowns and flashes of jewelry; waiting.

And Janiah waited with them. Nemesio had invited an eclectic mix to the opening. There were the inevitable media types lured in to ensure proper coverage. Given the exhibition, Janiah assumed there were also antique collectors there. President Nix was present, of course. He looked pleased at the prospect of being near so many potential donors, but also upset that they were not fawning all over him.

The lobby and exhibition room had been carefully prepped with discrete lighting and hors d'oeuvre tables. Janiah caught a glimpse of Pena brown-nosing the actor Michael Jai White and the rapper Wiz Khalifa. He looked flushed with pleasure at the way the evening was going, his long face nimbly registering sincerity, amusement, or respect as his various audiences required. Music could be heard faintly at times, but it was drowned out by the excited chatter coming from the affluent crowd. Waiters circulated with champagne in fluted glasses.

Amid the diamond sparkles, white teeth, and formal wear, the martial artists stood around, waiting.

"Pena looks pleased with himself," one of Divine Mathematics' other students said to Janiah as she sipped her mudslide. He was one of the newer trainees, and had volunteered to help out. Actually, there wasn't much to do, so he was enjoying champagne and the atmosphere.

"Pena doesn't have the good sense to be worried," Janiah said. "He smells money. It tends to cloud other issues."

"Like what?" the newer student asked and then he sipped some more of Pena's good champagne.

Janiah had been watching things for a while and had a whole mental list of things she was worried about. She just smiled at the student and shrugged, but deep down, she thought, *Money cloaks other things, like the smell of blood.*

Even before Janiah had arrived, she knew that the only thing the police had to go on was the martial arts link between both victims. Tony and James were still waiting for information about whether Wulff and Coutinho had connections to each other. But if she was right about 1488 choosing victims who were prestigious martial artists, then the presence of some of the area's most prominent martial artists would be irresistible. Tony's response to that was simply, "Oh boy, fresh meat."

Janiah thought about the real reason why the masters were there: they thought that 1488 was going to strike again… and soon. They weren't alone. What little Janiah had been able to find out from her brother suggested that the APD thought so, too. Everyone knew that 1488's last message meant that he wasn't done yet.

There was a fair amount of public pressure to solve the case. The potential for media hype was irresistible, and James' lieutenant had made it clear, in no uncertain terms, that things were not moving fast enough to satisfy the mayor, the commissioner, and the local news stations As a result, a whole team of detectives had been put on the job. James looked on it as less than an endorsement of his investigative skill.

To make things worse, the newspapers told Janiah that the Japanese community had posted a $40,000 reward for the return of the training sword. Tony and James thought the reward would draw every lunatic in the South and make their jobs that much harder. James was almost speechless with rage.

Tony's and James were at the museum, circulating discreetly around the fringes of the reception. Their suits were appropriately dark, but the wider jacket cut James needed for a shoulder holster tended to make that elegant cocktail-reception-look a hard one to achieve. Tony, on the other hand looked like a Black James Bond.

James' eyes swept over the crowd, groping for a subject. He looked tense. He was not really sure that 1488 would show, but he suspected that the mix of Pena's odd guest list and the pattern of 1488's crimes made it a good bet that something was going to go down. Besides, Tony had reminded Janiah that there was all that reward money.

As one of the participants in the museum's demonstration, Janiah was not really free to roam the party. She caught Tony's and James' eyes and jerked her head to one side to signal them to come over.

"Technically, I'm not even supposed to be here," James informed her. "Violation of Lieutenant Tat's orders. She wants me to rework the paper trail."

"Ooh, James," Tony crooned. "A violation. You gon' get in trouble."

James looked around. No one had noticed or overheard—the noise from the crowd had drowned Tony out.

"Hey, Mr. Mature... relax," James said.

"You relax," Tony shot back. "Pussy."

"Calling me a pussy isn't an insult fool," James said. "Pussy can take a beating and not get hurt, folks write songs and make movies about it, dudes will kill for it, and rich men will spend their last dollar for it."

"Asshole, then," Tony said.

"C'mon, y'all," Janiah said. "Let's keep it down."

You could see the muscles in Tony's neck and jaw work a little with the effort to suppress his frustration. He finally exhaled a long stream of air, like a pressure valve gradually bleeding the needle down off the red zone. "Okay," he sighed. "Okay."

"Look, I'm here, all right?" James said. "Get in trouble or not, I'm here. Friends to the end, T."

"Brothers," Tony said.

"Aw, how sweet," Janiah said with a smirk. "So what's the deal?"

"Three things," James answered, his index finger coming up. "One, if 1488 is stalking martial arts celebrities, he'll be here. Tonight's an opportunity for him to scope them out in the flesh. Probably too good to pass up. And if he's here, I want to see whether we can spot him."

"Probably a long shot," Tony grumbled. "I've gotta believe there's something else we don't see here. But what's the harm?"

"Other than to my career?" James said.

Touché, Tony said. "You're just a private citizens out for a night on the town, then; watching my little sister prance around like an extra in *Iron Fist*."

"*Iron Fist*?" Janiah said, frowning. "*Iron Fist* was lame. At least give me *Daredevil*... or even *Luke Cage*."

Tony eyed his sister's outfit. "You *are* flyer than these fools dressed in the ninja suits and the ones looking like Pai Mei from *Kill Bill*."

"Thanks, Tony." Janiah turned to James to pick up the thread of his analysis. "And what's the second reason you're here?"

"Two is that if there's some connection between the victims some of your martial arts masters know the reason, and they're just not telling us. We wanna scope 'em out."

"Come on," Janiah protested. "You really think the masters are holding out on you?"

James sighed. "First rule of being a cop: everybody lies."

Tony nodded. "And the third reason, is that nobody scoops me on a story. Nobody." He grinned as he said it, but there was no smile in his eyes.

Janiah looked at James with a raised eyebrow. He was grinning, too. His mouth and his eyes.

***

The crowd ebbed and flowed around tables of food and waiters bearing trays. Janiah stood near the performance area, trying not to let the atmosphere distract her. It was almost show time.

Pena's idea for the demonstration had been effectively vetoed by the masters, then hijacked by them. The masters had put together an impressive plan for the demo. Armed and unarmed systems would be featured. Respecting his age, experience and skill, Chanchai Chulalongkorn—the oldest and longest training master in the South—headed the list.

Chanchai Chulalongkorn was tiny, but hard as diamond and cut like jewelry. He was possessed of a gravity created by the accumulation of experience. He had a gray, flat-top buzz cut and a wide brow. His dark eyes peered over his high cheekbones. His lips were thin, and his honey-toned skin was extremely wrinkled, the only sign that he had been training for nearly sixty years. On his head he wore a gold mongkon—a type of braided headgear worn by Thai martial arts fighters and masters. The Mongkon was given to a student after their teacher saw that he or she had become an experienced fighter and learned a great deal of knowledge about their martial art.

Even Divine Mathematics respected the old Krabi-Krabong master. Krabi-Krabong was a weapon-based martial art from Thailand. The system's name referred to its main weapons, namely the Thai sword—*krabi*—and staff—*krabong*. Typically, a pair of swords was wielded. Unarmed Krabi-Krabong, called Muay Boran, made use of kicks, pressure point strikes, joint locks, holds, and throws. Chanchai was a master of the art and combined dignity and elegance with lightening fast reflexes.

Chanchai and Divine Mathematics, the most experienced master in Atlanta and the second or third most experienced in the South, were originally scheduled to open up the exhibition with a Thai swords versus machete demonstration, but to everyone's surprise, Divine Mathematics backed out and put Janiah in his place. He explained to the other masters that he had damaged the ulnar nerve in his right arm and would not be able to wield the machete correctly.

It was a valid excuse, Janiah supposed. The only problem was that Janiah had never seen Divine Mathematics with an injury as debilitating as that. And just that morning he had been going at it hard with two students.

The masters were annoyed. Divine Mathematics might have vouched for Janiah, but for such an important public display, her role was a cause for concern for the other masters.

So there was another thing that worried Janiah. Chanchai, all dressed up in his black silk top and short with red and gold accents to match his gold sash, was now being forced to work with what he considered to be an inferior product—her. Only his respect for Divine Mathematics and his need to maintain a dignified public appearance kept him from storming out of the room.

To make things more complicated, Janiah and Chanchai were going to be using live blades—sharp steel. Most times, they are unsharpened replica blades with the look and feel of a sword or machete but they could not cut. That night's performance, however, Janiah and the venerable master would be using real krabi and machete.

So... a big-ass crowd; the possible presence of a murderer; my brother about to explode; a deeply annoyed demo partner; and live swords," Janiah thought. *If I didn't have bad luck, I wouldn't have any luck at all.*

Divine Mathematics fussed over her, making sure her clothes were fitting right; that her shoes were tied tightly; that his machete, which he was letting her use, was polished and lightly oiled.

When Divine Mathematics knelt to remove the machete from the lacquered wooden rack it rested on, a buzz started as people thought the demonstration was about to begin. Divine Mathematics ignored them and went on with his work. Satisfied, he rose and crossed over to the other side of the area to speak briefly with Chanchai.

Janiah tried to stay calm. She watched the crowd, looking for anything unusual. *What does a killer look like, anyway?* She thought. She caught a sense of personalities in motion, brief glimpses. But any insight was lost in the crowd's motion.

Divine Mathematics returned to her. "We begin in ten minutes, Mack."

Janiah noticed that a small envelope had been left by Chanchai's sword stand while Janiah was distracted. Chanchai moved smoothly to the sword rack and picked up the note. He glanced at it and placed it inside his top. Then he picked up his swords. After taking a deep breath, Janiah followed suit.

The demonstration finally began. Janiah was relieved, because she could not deal with any more psychic clutter. There was a fanfare and some words of welcome. The mayor, who was up for reelection, had gotten wind of the press coverage, and she was there. Some extra verbiage was tossed around while Chanchai and Janiah edged over to the side of the performance area. The crowd clustered around and Janiah scanned their faces. She saw James, who winked at her, President Nix looked pleased. There were lots of strangers. Some looked distracted. Some looked bored. Some looked rich and quite a few looked drunk. But no one looked like a murderer.

The words bubbled away eventually. There was applause and then silence. Janiah and the old master were on.

The blade exchange was not choreographed. They would take turns attacking each other and countering the attack. They had agreed on five attacks each.

Janiah knew that there could be no hesitation in her actions, no flaw in her technique.

Just for kicks, Divine Mathematics had arranged for a cutting performance before the demo to show the audience that the blades were real. Chanchai and Janiah faced each other about twenty feet apart. Behind each of them and slightly to one side, three hunks of pork, each as thick as a man's neck, were driven atop poles.

At Divine Mathematics' command, Janiah and Chanchai strode forward, closing the gap between them and crossing to the opposite side. Janiah drew her machete and cut at the ham.

Janiah sliced though the hunks of pork, one after the other. As she spun to face Chanchai, the stumps that held the pork quivered and swayed slightly with the force of the attack. Then the severed top sections of ham fell to the floor with a thud.

The crowd went crazy. Janiah looked over at Tony and even he looked excited.

Chanchai smiled at Janiah then leapt high into the air. He spun and then quickly cut outward with both swords. All three pieces of severed pork fell to the floor just before he landed.

The crowd clapped, stomped and whistled.

A bead of sweat rolled down Janiah's forehead. She had never seen anyone execute a cut that fast with a sword.

Janiah raised her machete before her. Chanchai brought one sword up to the side of his ear and the other in front of his chest. They exploded toward each other.

Chanchai attacked first, slicing downward at the top of her head with both swords. Janiah evaded the blows by fading back just far enough for the cuts to miss.

Janiah slid forward and countered with a decisive slash to the neck.

Chanchai slowly raised the tip of his right sword toward Janiah's chest and held it aloft. Janiah understood and crossed her machete with his blade. Chanchai's sword and her machete felt held together by a magnetic force.

Chanchai thrust at her gut with the sword in his left hand.

Janiah pressed downward and to her right with the machete, blocking the thrust with Chanchai's right sword.

I was supposed to go that time, Janiah thought. *Is Chanchai really trying to hurt me?*

They broke apart and backed up to their initial starting points, eyeing each other warily.

Each of the attacks and counters that followed were just as fast, just as powerful, just as intense. When Janiah put the machete back in its sheath, the olive green 550 paracord wrapped around the handle was dark with perspiration.

When it was finally over and Janiah saluted Chanchai, she had no real idea how the audience thought they had done. In many ways, the reality of the crowd had faded for her during the demonstration and it seemed as if the universe was filled only by the blades, their points and edges, and the threatening deadliness of Chanchai's technique. Janiah had some vague memory of the crowd cheering, but that was it. Chanchai, it seemed to her, had not been as precise as Janiah would have expected, but it was only an impression of a microsecond's hesitation. Not something a casual viewer would have noticed.

The crowd applauded as Janiah followed Chanchai out of the performance area. She saluted Chanchai. Chanchai put his hands together like someone in prayer, then placed the sides of his index fingers to his forehead and brought his chin to his chest. "Sawadee khap," he said, thanking her in Thai.

Chanchai then turned and went to Divine Mathematics. He bowed to him and they spoke for a moment. Then Chanchai left. It was a surprise, but maybe he felt the need to get out of the area after what Janiah was sure he thought of as an embarrassing performance.

Janiah turned to watch the next demonstration. She spotted James and Tony, but they were looking at faces, focused on the performance area.

A noted karate master strode to the center of the performance area, capturing the crowd's attention. Muscular and confident, he bowed to the assembled masters. He stood silently for a moment, the breath coming and going with a tidal rhythm. His hands rose up in front of him higher than his head. The thumbs and forefingers of his open hands touched, making a triangle shape through which he looked for a moment.

Janiah felt a presence behind her. "Mack," Divine Mathematics whispered in her ear. "Something's up. Get your brother and his cop friend."

Janiah gathered with Divine Mathematics, Tony and James behind the audience, off in a corner. There were small clusters of people more interested in the free champagne than what was going on in the stage area. Back there, you could hear people talking and the occasional discreet laugh.

Tony and James listened quietly, still watching the crowd, as Divine Mathematics explained.

"Something's wrong. Chanchai—" He looked at

Janiah. "You noticed?"

"He wasn't as focused as I thought he would be," Janiah said.

Divine Mathematics nodded. "Exactly," Divine Mathematics said. He took two attacks in a row and there were moments where his awareness seemed clouded."

"He looked pretty cold-blooded to me," James said.

Divine Mathematics smiled. "Yeah, you wouldn't know good martial arts if it walked up to you and said, 'Hey, I'm good martial arts'," he said.

Janiah and James laughed.

"Is that all," Tony asked with some exasperation. "The old geezer was off his game?"

"Naw, son. That's not all." Divine Mathematics' tone was not something James was used to hearing from people, and he turned on him with the full power of his cop stare. Divine Mathematics did not flinch. "As he left, Chanchai apologized to me for his faltering performance." He turned to face Janiah. "He asked me to offer congratulations to you on the level of your skill, Mack."

"Yeah, yeah," Tony said, "Janiah's a regular whirlwind of death. Can we get to the point?"

Divine Mathematics was not used to being addressed like that, either. Janiah saw it in his eyes, but he went on. "Chanchai apologized and told me that he had received a note. And that he hoped to be able to redeem our honor tonight."

The only reason they were able to catch up with Chanchai at all was that he took a while to fold his formal uniform. Even with all that was on his mind, Chanchai was a methodical man. His uniform would be neatly folded, his other items carefully packed. He had spent a lifetime learning not to cut corners and that night was no exception.

Janiah spotted him as he left the dressing room. He was less conspicuous in his street clothes, as if they were designed to shield the world from seeing his true nature. He threaded through the crowd and headed out the door. Janiah headed out after him. She had watched men like Chanchai move for years and knew how deceptive he would be once he got going.

CHAPTER ELEVEN

The car, with its APD card on the dash, was parked in a 'No Parking' zone close to the Martial Masters entrance. Tony and Janiah piled in and they shot down the street.

"He just entered the parking garage," James reported as he ran back from the corner and then hopped into the seat beside Tony. Tony had the car in gear before James' door was even closed.

"Where's the exit?" Janiah's brother asked.

"Around the block." James picked up the radio's handset and asked for a record check for auto registration.

"Right or left?" Tony asked.

"Left," James replied

Tony raced the car across traffic. His high-speed turn made the tires squeal. The maneuver drew a few cranky horn blasts and threw Janiah up against the car door. James worked the radio like nothing was happening. He seemed to be glued to the seat. "How do you spell his name?" he asked me.

"What's he drive?" Tony demanded.

"A Volkswagen Beetle."

My brother grunted. "Figures."

The radio came to life. "VW Bug, matte black," James told Tony. He gave him the tag number and they scanned the road ahead. The garage was one of those multilevel affairs buried in the wall of buildings that lined the street. Cars sprang out of the gated exit directly into traffic, like rabbits from a hole. The night road ahead was flecked with red taillights. From the backseat, Janiah couldn't see their expression, but she could almost feel the eye strain as the two men peered into the distance to try to spot Chanchai. The tension evaporated and they both settled back into the seat with relief as the VW exited the garage.

"Okay," Tony said. "Here we go."

They trailed Chanchai through Atlanta's night traffic.

Tony was cursing softly under his breath, trying to stay close, but not too close, to Chanchai's car and avoid the vehicles that passed by. James quietly narrated their progress across town. Janiah noticed that they did not bicker at all.

They were headed to Alpharetta.

"He live up here?" James asked Janiah. Janiah shook her head.

"So what's in Alpharetta?" Tony asked. "Chanchai have a school there?"

"Nope," Janiah replied.

"And he doesn't live there?" James reconfirmed. All

Janiah could do was shake her head. "Okay, no problem," he said.

Tony shot Janiah a quick side-eye. "Shit, shit, shit," he spat. "I told you these dudes were holding out on you, James."

"Many Thai live up that way," Janiah suggested lamely.

Tony edged a little closer to the Volkswagen, muscling his way through the close-packed lanes. He didn't want to lose Chanchai.

Tony jockeyed around in the middle lane, swinging his head quickly over his right shoulder to check the blind spot in case they had to go in that direction. "So what do you think, James?" Tony asked.

"I don't think he's going home. I think he's got a meeting set up."

"Me, too," Tony said.

"Why?" Janiah asked.

"Think about it," Tony said. "If you were gonna try to catch this dude, where would you look, Janiah?"

"I guess I'd stake out a martial arts school."

"Correct," James chimed in. "And why is that?"

"Because... I guess because the other murders took place in martial arts schools, or places like them."

"Right." Tony said with a nod. "And the one thing that trips most murderers up, James?"

"Pattern. Predictability," James said.

"So, sis," Tony continued, "We got your teacher's pal shooting out of the reception like his ass is on fire. A mysterious message that obviously got to him. And now he's heading somewhere. Not home. Something's going down."

"Maybe," Janiah said grudgingly. She was still trying to digest the swirl of action that had not seemed to let up since Chanchai and her crossed swords for the demonstration.

"1488 has got to know somebody's looking for him," James said.

"He may be crazy," Tony said.

"But he's not dumb," James finished.

"So, after all the publicity in the papers, he's got to find another spot to get at his victim," Tony said. "Now that you think about it, maybe the whole Martial Masters reception looked to him like a great way to get us looking in the wrong place."

"Yep," James said with a nod. "And while we're all tied up there, he sets up another location."

"But he's got to have a way to lure somebody to the meet," Tony said. "I wonder what he's got?"

"Gotta be some powerful mojo," James said. "He's already used it on two others."

Janiah nodded in affirmation. Part of her was wondering whether her brother had not been right all along: the masters knew something they were not telling. Janiah had the sickening feeling that maybe *her* teacher knew something.

The Beetle made a quick right turn. They kept pace.

"Mr. Man, Mr. Man, where are you heading?" Tony said under his breath

Chanchai took a left. It led along a strip of park lined with trees whose bark was mottled like camouflage. The chain-link fencing around the park's playground was ten feet high. Iron swing sets and monkey bars made odd shapes in the darkness. A squat brick Parks Department building stood in the middle of the grass strip. Passing headlights revealed colorful graffiti on the building's walls.

A left again, then a right.

Chanchai slowly rolled down a one-way side street. Small factories and warehouses dotted the street, shuttered tight and washed in the odd light of sodium lamps. There were narrow garages there as well, former stables from the 1920s that had been converted for cars. The block ended ahead.

"What's the deal here, Janiah?" They were not too far from where Janiah used to live before relocating to the much cheaper West End and Tony was relying on her for some information.

"The street dead-ends. Not much over here. A few shops around the corner."

Chanchai pulled over and they followed suit, farther back on the block. Tony turned off the headlights and they watched.

The Beetle's lights went out. Chanchai got out of the car. He took a quick glance around, sweeping the shadows. His eyes were dark slashes in the sodium wash of the streetlight. Janiah shrunk back into the seat almost involuntarily. She knew the man and what he was capable of. She felt as if he had sensed their presence, but it did not seem to bother him. He popped the trunk and removed something long and narrow from the car, then began walking toward the corner.

Tony gestured. "What?" he asked his sister quietly.

Janiah let out a tense breath. "It's a sword bag."

"It's happening, Tony said, his voice sharp with excitement. "What's there?" he pointed as Chanchai turned right at the corner.

"Nothing," Janiah said. "It's blocked off for construction."

"C'mon, y'all," James said. "Time's wasting. Something's there."

"Nothing," Janiah said again. Then it came to her. "Wait... there's an old entrance to the old Alpharetta subway stop."

"In use?" Tony had already started to roll the car forward.

"No," Janiah replied. "It's closed down."

They looked quickly at each other. "Perfect," James said. He reached under his coat and checked his pistol then he handed Tony a two-way radio and Tony squelched it for a test.

"There's an exit further ahead?" James asked.

"Next block," Janiah said.

Things were beginning to speed up and the conversation, the movements, everything had the feeling of getting tight.

"Okay." James was doing three things at once. Checking his gun. Handling the radio. Undoing the seat belt. His brain had to be racing. "I'll go in here. You block the other exit?" He looked at Tony for confirmation.

Tony nodded in agreement and they rolled ahead to the corner where Chanchai had turned right. James leapt out the door. Chanchai was nowhere to be seen. Across the street, the closed subway entrance was dark. An old sign, dirty with time and neglect, hinted faintly at the old platform's presence. One of those old metal turnstiles marked the entrance. James shined a flashlight on the entrance. A chain hung from the turnstile, swaying slightly. The light picked up the fresh cut where the links had been severed. James gave Tony and Janiah a last look, nodded, then followed Chanchai into the shadows that led down into the subway.

"Shit, James," Tony said to the night where his best friend had been.

Tony sped the car toward the other end of the station, but never made it.

James' voice crackled over the two-way radio. "Tony," he whispered cautiously. Then louder, more urgently, "Tony!"

Tony jerked the car to a stop and sprung out, the door hanging open. Janiah's window was closed but the sound of the gunshot was clear as it punched its way up from the old platform. Janiah snapped her head in its direction.

Tony sprinted around the front of the car and headed for the subway turnstile. His gun—a monstrous .500 S&W revolver gifted to him by James on his 35th birthday a year ago—was out and he was calling into his radio: "James?

James?"

Janiah sat for a moment, watching things unfold with a bewildering quickness. Janiah popped the car door open, unsure of what to do next. The engine was still running and the keys glinted in the darkness, dancing with vibration. The radio mounted on the dash chattered. Janiah got out of the car and headed toward her brother.

Tony hit the entranceway and, from down in the subway, a muffled string of concussions thudded into the night.

Things were bad.

The turnstile entrance was dark and the metal moaned as Janiah moved through it. The brief corridor smelled of damp concrete and urine. Janiah hurried onto the stairs leading down to the old station.

A hundred yards to her left, the platform was brightly lit. But there, it was dim. Janiah took the stairs as fast as she could. The steps were slick with dead leaves and old newspapers.

Janiah did not know what to expect—movement, some kind of action. She could sense faint forms huddled at the bottom of the landing.

She could also smell the scent of gunfire in the air. She could also smell the dankness. And something else that she could not identify yet. She could hear the faint hum of the traffic up above in the distance. Then Janiah picked up an odd buzzing noise racing through the metal rails on the subway tracks that told you a train was approaching. But there was something else as well, another noise Janiah could not immediately identify.

As Janiah got closer, cutting through the

background noise, small, liquid gasps floated up into the night air from below her.

A southbound train sped by. Its light washed the scene. Janiah spotted Chanchai crouched in a corner, gripping the handle of his sword. His face was a mask of anger, rigid and intense. He tried to say something as Janiah slid down the stairs, but the noise of the speeding train swallowed it.

Then she knew what she smelled.

In the strobe like flutter of the light from the train cars, Tony knelt in a black pool of blood that washed across the platform. In his arms, James lay stretched out. It was dark, but Janiah could see his handless wrist where blood pulsed out onto the concrete. His shirt was dark and slick from a deep gash across his torso. He was sliding deep down into shock and gazing up frantically as if trying to pierce the night sky for a last glimpse of the world. His face was straining in the effort. James gulped spasmodically at the air, his lips working in frantic haste.

The noise of the train passed and Janiah could hear Tony screaming at her, "Put some pressure on it, God dammit!" He jerked his chin at the gushing arm. Then into the radio he shouted, "Officer down! Officer down!" In the rapid pattern of darkness and light thrown by the train, Tony looked wild, caught up in a mix of rage, frustration and despair.

1488 was nowhere to be seen. In the distance, a siren whooped, its frantic call a faint offer of hope.

Janiah knelt across from her brother and pressed down hard on James' arm. "Hang on, bruh," Tony said. "Hang on." Tony rocked back and forth, cradling James' head in one hand, working the radio with the other.

The sirens got closer. Janiah could hear shouts. People were moving cautiously down toward them from the lighted platform.

James seemed to seize up; his back arched and he made choking sound. Tony dropped the radio and held him tight. James' face calmed a bit as if reassured. It was hard to tell at that point if he was even aware of them. Janiah felt like something essential had just been wrenched from her, deep down in her guts. Janiah looked about in that dark place, searching for help. It seemed to take a long time to come. Janiah turned back to face her brother.

Even in the washed out light of that place, the tears in Tony's eyes glittered.

CHAPTER TWELVE

When James married Fatou, he converted to Islam. Not the Arab way of practicing, but the African way, particularly the way of the Wolof of Senegal, which still kept some of the traditional ways of the Wolof people. So amid the tubes and beeping machines of the ICU, there were the whispered Muslim prayers and traditional rituals performed by a marabout—a Muslim leader, teacher and diviner. The man was young for a marabout—in his late thirties or early forties. He sat uncomfortably with everyone in the waiting room, ready to speak and eager to comfort. He took a look at Tony and at the police who had come to be with the family. They were hard-faced men. The marabout wisely squashed his impulse to tell everyone about the beneficence and mercy of Allah. No one was in the mood for it.

Fatou sniffed once or twice but held it together. Aisha sat with her. James' daughter, red-eyed and washed out, stared at a world that had been blown apart and revealed as the uncertain place it really was. It was a hard thing to learn at nine years of age. At any age.

The doctors could not say whether James would make it. Family and friends waited around the hospital, not saying much. They were a tight knot of people hesitant to come to grips with the grim possibilities before them. It had been a long night, but it seemed like there were better things to do than just wait. The police set up shifts: some stayed; some went back out on the streets. After a while, Janiah emerged into the bright sunlight, blinking with the suddenness of the glare and the harsh, relentless way of the world.

The ride home was a leaden progression through different mental landscapes. The growing summer heat blazed through the windshield, fighting with the air conditioner for dominance. It added to the general feeling of impending disaster. For distraction, Janiah watched the scenery rush by, but it did not work. Her eyes were open, but Janiah was really just seeing the aftermath of that night.

A transit police officer at the next station had heard the shots and called for backup—the radios Tony and James were using were encrypted sets that could not reach the police communication network. A car from the local precinct was the first on the scene, both police officers from the cruiser nervously waving guns and lights around until they were sure who all the people present were. By that time, Chanchai had joined Janiah by James' side, which was a good thing; if he'd still been crouched in the corner with a sword, the police would have killed him for sure.

The ambulance got there at about the same time. Two beefy men in tailored uniform shirts snapped on latex gloves and got to work. They surveyed the scene and knelt down across from Tony.

"Shit," one gasped. He was looking at the mess of James' chest and his stump, trying to figure out what to do first. You could see the judgment in his eyes like a shutter flickering, but his hands never stopped moving. "Shock suit," he told his partner.

Tony's voice was flat and far away. "He's already bled out."

The EMT nodded in acknowledgment. "Maybe. Maybe not. We gotta try, man," he said gently. "Hey," he shouted at one of the police officers. "Put that piece away and find the hand, then bag it in ice."

The police holstered their guns sheepishly and did what the EMT said.

Then he began with the tools at his disposal—tubes; shock suit; blood expanders. They trundled James out of the subway and away with grim, firm moves, a show of aid performed in equal parts for the victim and the witnesses. The ambulance whooped away into the night.

Then Chanchai and Janiah got hustled off the subway platform and back up to street level. The area was thick with police cars, lights flashing rapidly around the site. Radios crackled and sputtered and police officers rushed back and forth, frantic to impose some sense of order on the jumble of witnesses and blood and darkness.

Janiah, Tony and Chanchai were escorted to the nearest police station. No one there was happy to see them. A police officer walked them into the main room and silently put Chanchai's sword on a desk. It was wrapped in brown paper and tagged. Then Chanchai and Janiah were split up and the desk sergeant told someone to put them in interrogation rooms.

Janiah heard Tony's voice in the hall asking where Chanchai was. The door to her room opened and Tony stuck his head in. His expression was hard. His only comment was, "Fox cleared my name. What a cluster fuck.

Sit tight." Then he was gone. He must have identified Janiah to the people at the precinct; things got a little less tense. But a police officer was down, and the fluorescent lights did little to dispel the dinginess of the station or the somber tone of the interrogation.

Chanchai was still gray-faced and silent when they led him away. After Janiah had her statement taken, several different detectives came in and asked her the same series of questions over and over again. They had a real knack for making a person feel like they were lying, even when they were telling the truth.

It was after two A.M. before Janiah saw Chanchai again. He looked old. His face was a wall; only his eyes moved behind it. The sensei sat in a chair with his hands cupped in his lap, palms up.

Janiah sat next to him, watching the ebb and flow of a police station at night. She did not look at Chanchai. But when he spoke his voice was so low that she had to so she could read his lips.

"He was waiting there," the old man murmured. "In the dark. The note I received said that he would be." He inhaled deeply. "I was not sure it would be so.

"It was a narrow space," he went on, his right hand stirring faintly in his lap, as if coming alive with the retelling. "Dark. Dirty. Janiah, it was not a place... of honor."

What did you say? Janiah wanted to ask. But she was afraid the sound of her voice would ruin Chanchai's story. His eyes were not focused on the room, but peered back into the subway.

"He told me it was regrettable but could not be

avoided." Chanchai paused while the wheel of memory turned for him. "I told him I was there to accept his challenge. He seemed surprised. But he understood courtesy, that one. We bowed. It was a narrow place.

"I circled away from the stairs toward the wall," he said, his hand shaking even more. "It was dark, but I could feel him watching me. By the wall, I could look out and the light around him made him a better target." He smiled. "We drew our swords. His sword draw was.. strong. I believe the Japanese call it 'nukitsuke'." For him to classify 1488's sword drawing as strong told Janiah volumes.

"Then the policeman came. The big one who looks like Michael Ealy, from *Being Mary Jane*—that's my show."

James Pedersen," Janiah said.

"I do not believe Officer Pedersen even saw me in the shadows," Chanchai went on. "He came down the stairs so fast, he had little time. Just some words in the radio." He took a breath to continue, then paused as if editing his thoughts, "The stairs were slippery. The platform too. I called out a warning to the policeman—

"The... man... he turned on the policeman and cut him. The gun went off." Chanchai paused as if the memory of the shot punctuated his narrative. "I saw the rage in his eyes by the light from the gun's flash. It was like the heat of a furnace, his anger."

Chanchai sat forward with the tension, then relaxed a bit. "He struck the policeman's wrist," the old man said. Janiah knew that the wrist cut was one of the most common used in kendo. "He cut his right hand. In the dark, it looked as if the policeman had a gun in it."

But James is left-handed, Janiah thought.

Chanchai continued. "The first shot came as the blade sliced down." Janiah could imagine the flash of gunfire and the glitter of the blade's arc. "It froze the swordsman for a moment."

And that pause was probably why James was not dead.

"But the swordsman recovered," Chanchai said. "He was quick, that one." He stopped again, caught in the vividness of his memory. "I began to move, but he had already crossed to the other side. I could not get a clear strike. He moved in.

"I am not sure what technique he used then," Chanchai said apologetically, as if identifying the simple mechanics could change the ultimate outcome of that night.

"But he took the gun away from the big one... the rest you know."

Janiah and Chanchai sat in the white noise of the station and remembered the sound of the shots, a string of muffled blasts that 1488 squeezed off, the pistol muzzle searching for James' side like an open mouth.

Janiah nodded. The rest she knew.

Later that day, after the vigil at the ICU, Janiah drove out to Tony's house. She had spoken to her brother in private only briefly since the night James was wounded. He was monosyllabic and distant, on a break from the case, as were all reporters—until APD and Internal Affairs had investigated the incident in the subway.

Even as night approached, the sun hammered down, not letting up. Tony's children were in the pool, paddling around and playing with face masks and little plastic boats.

Aisha was out there, a faint sheen of perspiration on her flushed face, trying to keep them quiet.

Janiah came through the fence and around the house to the pool side.

"Hey, Aisha," Janiah said. Tony's wife smiled at her and the children waved. She watched them splash around for a bit. "Is Tony around?"

Aisha stared at Janiah. She looked beat too, but her high cheekbones stood out with a type of false vitality. "Sort of," she said. "He's in the family room." She picked up a glass and sucked at a straw and watched Janiah walk up to the sliding doors.

The room was dark. Janiah put her face up to the screen and peered in. She glimpsed a suggestion of motion and heard the faint clink of ice cubes. The thunk of a glass being set down on a wooden table.

"What?" He said, his voice raspy.

Janiah slid the screen over and stepped inside. Tony was holed up in the gloom like an animal in a cave. Janiah pulled a chair over and sat down without saying anything. He got up and fumbled in the dark, set a glass down on the table in front of her, tossed some ice cubes into it, and poured her a drink. In the dark it was hard to tell, but as Janiah lifted the glass up she could smell the Irish whiskey.

He settled back in the chair like an old man and tipped his glass at her in a toast.

Janiah swirled the glass around, making the cubes clink. She took a sip and watched him. "Have you been in here long?" she asked.

"A while."

Janiah listened to him carefully, but he was doing a good job getting his tongue around the words. He was still sober.

"Got a plan?" Janiah asked.

He reached over and turned on a light. Tony's normally bright eyes were dark, like pieces of stone.

"Of course, I do," Tony said. "I'm gonna squeeze your man, Divine Mathematics until he pops."

"What?"

Tony took a hit of his drink. You could hear him inhale as he brought the glass to his lips. He squinted at Janiah as the whiskey went down. "I told you there was something going on with those martial arts freaks... that includes your teacher."

"You got anything that proves it?" Janiah asked. "I mean, other than some hunch?"

"My hunches pay off, sis."

"Look, just because you're coming up empty doesn't mean that Divine Mathematics, or any other martial arts master, is involved."

"Oh no?"

"No," Janiah said.

"Well, you tell me how this fits together." He sloshed some more whiskey into the glass. The lamp glowed through the greenness of the Redbreat's whiskey bottle. "You got a major homicide here. One in New Orleans and another in Austin. Same martial arts MO. Then, last night, who gets a meeting set up with the killer? Your teacher." He glared at Janiah.

"What are you talking about?" Janiah hissed. "It was Chanchai who got the note."

Tony gave Janiah a side-eye. "Damn, Dumb and Dumber, think... your teacher was scheduled to do the demo. The note was for him. Chanchai picked it up by mistake."

Janiah thought for a minute. "Okay, when you string things together like that, it sounds plausible, but, look, we know that whoever's doing this has some sort of martial arts fixation and a racist. I mean, the whole '1488' thing... the theft of the bokken. Don't you think it's possible that Divine Mathematics got singled out just because he's a prominent martial arts master *and* Black?"

"You still working that martial arts Stan angle, Janiah? It's thin."

"No thinner than you trying to pin Divine Mathematics for something he's not involved in."

Tony looked hard at her. "You sure of that, Janiah?"

Janiah thought of Divine Mathematics. His silences and the sense she had of trying to break through a shield any time she looked at him. His unpredictable nature. The ways in which he made people feel both awe and fear, often simultaneously. Janiah nodded.

"I'd know Tony. He wouldn't hide something like this from me. It's too important."

"Everybody lies and everybody keeps secrets, Janiah," Tony said. "Even your teacher."

"You don't know him."

"Little sis, don't be fooled," Tony said. "You think he's so special—" The contempt in his voice was palpable.

"Fuck you, Tony."

"Fuck you, Janiah."

Janiah waited. All she got was sullen silence. The cubes rattled as Tony drank.

"This ain't gonna help with anything," she finally said. "You got anything else?"

"Not yet."

"Any new leads?"

"Hey, I'm working on it," he snapped. My other sources on APD are checking some things out for me."

"You're not working on anything but a hangover," Janiah said.

Tony gave no response.

"You gonna let this guy walk? After what he did to James?" Janiah asked.

"No one's gettin' away," Tony said.

"Then what?" Janiah said.

He waved his glass vaguely. "I got some things to work on."

Then Tony seemed to deflate a bit in the chair and he mumbled something at her.

"What," Janiah said.

Tony leaned forward and said something, but it was

low and to himself.

"What, " Janiah insisted." What did you say?"

"Nothing," Tony said.

Janiah did not know what she was angrier at, the whole situation, Tony's accusation of Divine Mathematics, the fact she had to defend him, or the nagging doubt that she felt. Something gave inside her. She stood up, reached down, and grabbed Tony by his lapel.

"Tell me what you just said, god dammit!"

Janiah must have touched something raw and hurtful way down inside him. He jumped to his feet. Janiah heard the bottle of whiskey flip over. Janiah was not expecting the sudden move and fell backward, tripping over a piece of furniture in the dim room. She sat sprawled on the floor as Tony stood swaying over her, furious.

"Don't push it, Janiah! You and all that martial arts bullshit. I should have had myself more together, but I was too busy paying attention to you."

"What do you mean?" Janiah asked.

"You asshole! I never should have let you come along last night," Tony said.

"What?"

"Don't you get it?" he yelled. "James had vests in the trunk! He had vests in the trunk and I forgot to make him put one on!"

Janiah thought for a minute that he was going to attack her. Then he retreated back into himself, collapsing into the chair. Janiah looked at him in the silence and slowly got to her feet.

Tony had the hard-edged fatalism of a crime reporter. He knew, more often than not, that the worst thing that can happen usually does. You hear about the guilt of survivors. Veteran soldiers and anyone that works on the sharp end of things knows about it. The feeling that you could have, should have done more, or something else, to stave off the disaster. It does not matter whether someone is just wounded or blown away. Whatever the event, you still get the intimate revelation of your own mortality. The secret joy that it was not you whose number was up. All those feelings get mixed into an acidic stew of guilt that can eat away at you, drop by drop, over days, or years, or a lifetime.

Janiah took a deep breath and tried again. "That's crap and you know it, T. It's not my fault. And it's not your fault either." Tony did not respond. "We didn't do anything wrong. 1488 did," she said.

Tony just grunted.

"You know James doesn't blame you," she said.

Tony just sat there and Janiah went on. "Do you think if your positions were reversed that James would do what you're doing? Blaming yourself? Feeling sorry for yourself? A guy like that?"

Tony leaned toward her, his face ghosting into the shadow thrown by the lamp. "Don't tell me what kind of guy he is," he said. "I know."

"Yeah. Even last night he was trying to tell us something," Janiah said." She remembered his mouth moving frantically; him gasping as he struggled unsuccessfully to talk.

Tony inhaled deeply and looked at her like he was both surprised and disappointed. "Janiah, James just had some fuckin' nut job try to empty the whole clip of a 9mm into him. You think he was together enough to send a message?"

Tony gave a harsh snort. "He was making noises, but they were just sounds. James' brain was already shutting down. His body just hadn't caught on."

Janiah did not believe that, mostly because she could not face it. Janiah still held out hope. So did the surgeons; every day James hung on was a good sign. Tony and Janiah sat for a while longer, looking out into the yard where the night grew stronger with each passing minute. The children's voices drifted in, muted sounds from another world. Tony sat there like a stone.

Janiah finished the whiskey and set the glass down next to her brother then rose and walked away. As she got to the screen, she paused and turned.

"I love you, Tony," Janiah said. She got nothing from him in response. "I love you, big brother."

Through the screen, Janiah could see Aisha toweling the children off as they came out of the pool. The image was softened by the filtering of the screen door and the arrival of full darkness. Janiah looked back into the room one last time.

"We're going to have to get him, Tony. It's personal, now." Janiah said it softly hoping for a reply. Ice cubes tinkled softly. Janiah went outside, closed the sliding screen door, and walked away.

***

Janiah went home and sat alone in her apartment.

It was hot. The side windows in the cottages that lined the block had fans or air conditioners in them. Janiah sat down in her memory foam floor chair. She closed her eyes and waited for calm. For insight. For a plan.

What she got were mental images of the subway platform. Of James. Of Chanchai. Of her brother drinking in the dark.

Her house was the place where Janiah slept, wrote and prepped meals for the *Urban Vegan* show. Janiah looked over toward the corner in her dining room where she did work or checked the internet on her laptop. The nearby walls were lined with books and papers. She studied African, Asian and Western history and world history. Did she do it because the past was safe? A place you could observe without being responsible for it? You could argue about its interpretation, sure. But you never had to really act to shape its outcome. Divine Mathematics had taught her that of all spheres of life, history best rewards your research.

And what about her and his arts? The African martial arts were highly effective, but archaic, a step removed from things. Even 52 Blocks was developed on the streets of New York and further developed in New York prisons long ago. Janiah trained, day after day, in the warrior arts of days long past, the urgent moves of battles lost or won decades, or even centuries ago. She was a warrior who never waged war, the disciple of a teacher who hid as much as he revealed.

And now she was confronted with all the things she had worked so hard to elude. Questions of trust. Of responsibility. Of life and death.

But Janiah knew one thing with a certainty: she was afraid.

A breeze stirred and moved the curtains. She stood, savoring it for a moment, then went to bed. The only insight she was left with was the one she had given Tony earlier: it was personal now.

CHAPTER THIRTEEN

Hoodoo Doctors chant in the dark to summon the dead. People have peered into the depths of caves for thousands of years, hoping the voice that sounded from the blackness could tell them the future.

It had rained in the night. When Janiah went for her jog at Stone Mountain, the morning sun made the blacktop of the pathway steam. The air was warm and thick with a rich mixture of dust, dew, and freshly cut grass. The day was heating up and the moist air was thickening. Janiah jogged along, trying to think of nothing. Instead, she thought of everything.

She was none the wiser for the experience.

***

There was a knock on the door. Aisha stood there with her husband.

"Is he sober, Aisha?" Janiah asked. She laughed and gestured at him.

Tony looked miserable. He squinted at her. "What kind of fucking question is that?" Tony said.

"A good one. Are you?"

"Well, I'm a little under the weather."

"Under the weather? That's one way of putting it," Janiah said. "Daddy always used to say he had 'the funk.'"

"I might have that, too," Tony moaned.

"Ignore him," Aisha said. "He's just being a baby."

Tony carried a box up into the house. It contained James' copies of the 1488 case files. Tony wasn't supposed to have them, but his connects in APD, some high-ranking officers, wanted to see James get justice. Justice they might have their hands to tied, or too many eyes on them, to bring.

Tony sat down, huffing in a chair. Aisha put a six-pack of Coke directly in front of him. Tony pulled a can off and held the cold aluminum to his forehead for a minute. Then he popped the tab. "We need to look at all this stuff, Janiah. Think about some things."

Aisha helped her uncrate the files. Tony sat in a chair, sipping the Coke.

"Here's what we've got," he began. "Chanchai's statement confirms that this guy is middle-aged and, despite the white supremacist shit, he's Asian. Apparently, a couple of the white supremacist groups let Asians in—the Proud Boys and Patriot Prayer, in particular. Even a couple of dumb ass Black Hispanics and a Samoan have joined up."

"Not surprising," Janiah said. "There's always been self-hating nuts out there. Did you talk with Chanchai again?"

"Not yet. I'm on leave, remember?" Tony seemed like he wanted to say more about it, but went off on a different tangent. "We don't know what would have ultimately happened the other night, but the MO seems the same. I gotta assume this guy is our killer."

Janiah nodded.

"DNA samples from the other crimes match up."

"The police never got any fingerprints that they could check from Martial Masters, did they?" Janiah asked.

He sat back again with his eyes closed. "Naw." It seemed like the word took a lot of effort.

What about... the gun," Janiah asked. She meant James' gun, but could not bring herself to say it.

Tony opened his eyes and looked at her. "They got partial prints. They're still running 'em down. Right now, we got zip. And we can't go through Interpol without James. I got no contacts there."

Remembering James made her think of his advice: "When you hit a wall, you go in a different direction."

Janiah sat down across from her brother. "What was it James said trips most killers up, Tony? Pattern?"

He nodded. "Yeah. And predictability."

"So what do we have here?" Janiah asked softly, because he had winced at the sound of her voice. "What's the pattern?"

Tony made a concerted effort to pull himself together. The copies of the file were spread out on the coffee table. Tony started to gingerly push the papers around. Aisha silently offered him a fresh Coke. Out of his vision, she put a hand to her lips and warned Janiah into silence.

Tony moved slowly at first. He began pulling things out and making groupings, pausing to sip at his drink frequently. Gradually, the tempo built up. Papers got arranged, spun around, compared. His watery, bloodshot eyes moved from spot to spot. He sat back and covered his face with his hands.

Tony gestured at the reports. "It's always the same. He's into this martial arts shit. You look at the list, and all the victims are connected by the arts. And killed by them."

"The pattern holds with Chanchai," Janiah said. "The other victims were somehow ambushed or lured into some sort of duel. And as far as we can tell, the victims had no connection to the killer."

"That we know," Tony said.

"And neither does Divine Mathematics," Janiah said.

Tony made a face. "Bullshit. You gotta start thinking clearly about this, sis."

"Okay, okay," Aisha said to calm them. "At least we agree that the link is martial mastery." They both looked at her. "I mean, it's obvious. Most of the guys he killed or tried to kill were martial arts masters, not green belts or some shit."

"Mejia's the exception," Janiah said. "He had a black belt, but he was nowhere near a master. He probably had less experience than me."

"Mejia's also unusual in that there was a theft associated with that homicide," Tony added. Janiah could tell that he wasn't letting go of the whole topic of Divine

Mathematics.

"Well, they're all into the martial arts," Aisha continued. "And this guy is... I dunno, tracking them down. Looking for something."

"And the trail leads here," Tony said quietly. "The messages at the crime scenes tell us that. There's gotta be a connection between the victims. And 1488's looking for another one here. So maybe the master theory is right. He murdered Mejia, but maybe he wasn't enough. There's something we don't see. Something right under our noses."

"Come on," Janiah said, knowing where he was headed, "Not that angle again."

"If the shoe fits, wear it," he said with rising conviction. "You may not want to hear it, but there's something your teacher ain't telling us."

Janiah took a deep breath and tried to stay calm. She remembered the debate the night before. "Okay, lay it out for me again, Tony."

He shrugged. "Seems obvious. 1488's after somebody in Atlanta. Somebody linked to the victims in New Orleans and Austin. Mejia wasn't the one, so let's think about it." His voice was getting stronger and harder as the words began to match the quickening cadence of his thoughts.

"All the victims are martial artists," Aisha offered. "All masters, except Mejia."

"Good chance whomever he's hunting now will be a master, too." Tony eyed Janiah.

"Okay, what other links do we have?" Janiah asked.

"Both Wulff and Coutinho were at the top of their

game."

"They were pretty well known. In the public eye," Janiah said. "You could see how they'd be chosen."

"True," he said. "But look at it from a slightly different angle. Let's assume we got a Japanese national, traveling alone, looking for somebody. He's stopping off at various cities. With the first two victims, we don't see much time wasted in terms of the homicides. 1488 kills Wulff in New Orleans and within a few days he shows up in Austin and snuffs Coutinho. Then he breaks into the Martial Masters museum, grabs some wooden sword, and smokes Mejia. But he hangs around. Why?"

Janiah thought it through. "Because Mejia was not who he was after."

"Maybe Mejia was part of the message," Aisha said quietly. "Or maybe he just got in the way. I mean, why steal the sword?"

"It pissed off the local masters pretty well," Tony said. "And it belonged to a famous Black samurai. Maybe that was the whole point." He sat back again and sipped at his Coke, his eyes far away. "Think about it like an ancient hunter after a leopard. They're not sure where the leopard is, so they send guys out into the bush to make a racket." He looked at Janiah for help.

"Beaters," Janiah said.

"Right. They do something to flush the leopard out of the grass."

"Are you telling me that the whole thing with Mejia was done just to get a reaction out of somebody?" Janiah said. "Come on."

"Yeah, I am," Tony said with conviction. "The theft wouldn't have made any kind of splash—some old wooden sword. But you link it with a killing and the papers are all over it," The expression on Tony's face was dead certain.

"I don't think Mejia's murder was a coincidence," he continued. "It was designed for effect. Just like with the first two. And the next time, the attempt in the subway, that was no fluke either." He looked up at Janiah. "Except his message got crossed and he ended up with the wrong master."

"There are alternative explanations," Janiah said. "There has to be."

"Bullshit," Tony said.

"I can't believe Divine Mathematics has anything to do with this," Janiah said.

"Bull. Shit." Tony repeated.

Aisha snorted in amusement at the two of them. "Look, how long will you two go around and around like this?"

They both shrugged.

"Janiah, I know you don't like to hear it, but think it through," Aisha said.

Janiah opened her mouth to speak, but Aisha smiled and went right on. "No, no, no. It's my turn," she said. "Let's go with your idea that your teacher isn't involved."

Janiah nodded in eager agreement.

"Okay, but we agree that the murderer is looking for someone, right?" Aisha said. "At the first murder scene in

New Orleans, were there signs of a search? Same in Austin?"

Tony looked through the reports. "Yep."

"Okay," Aisha said. "The killer's looking for someone. He doesn't know where he is. The first two victims weren't random. They somehow gave 1488 clues. They lead him 'the A', but he doesn't know where, exactly his target is. And so maybe he comes here to find out. And tries to do it through this Mojito guy."

"Mejia," Janiah said, correcting her.

"Whatever," Aisha said. "He was a pretty big martial arts name?"

Janiah nodded.

"You'd expect him to know things? Know people?"

Janiah nodded again.

"So there you go: this guy that the killer is looking for is like the other victims, except Mojito. A martial arts master. He's really good but really hard to find. The killer wanted Mojito to tell him."

Janiah started to get an uncomfortable feeling, a vague tingling. Aisha seemed unaware of the effect of her words on her. She flashed an *Inside Kung-Fu* at her. "There's an article here about martial arts in Nigeria. A part is about a force of war chiefs that protect the people."

Aisha showed her a picture. "Did you see this picture?"

It was a painting of the ancient Eso of the Yoruba people—seventy war chiefs, called Balogun, who follow the

War Chiefs of War Chiefs, the Aare Ona Kakanfo.

"They're pretty distinctive because they're uniforms are navy blue," Janiah said. "I think the other warriors wore red.

"So work this angle," Aisha said. "I mean, come on, who you do know among the martial artists in Atlanta that's a master *and* hard to find." She waved the picture at me. "And always dresses in navy blue like these guys?"

Janiah stayed quiet because she did not want to have to give his name.

Tony rubbed his temples with his fingers and watched her. He poked at the paper on the table in front of him. Gregoire's notes were there. "First, Wulff in New Orleans," he said.

"Then Coutinho in Austin," Tony added, with a bit more energy.

"So who's next," Tony asked. "New Orleans, Austin—" He let the question hang in the air.

And, after a time, the answer struck her. "Atlanta. 561,"

Tony stared at Janiah with a raised eyebrow. "That mean something, Janiah?"

"It's supreme mathematics from the Five Percenters," Janiah admitted slowly, with growing dismay. "Divine Mathematics' only sibling was his little sister people called R-E-K, or 'Wreck'. Refinement Equality Knowledge."

"There's the pattern," Tony said. "Hell '1488' itself is a number that represents words, too."

"But what about Mejia?" Janiah pointed out.

"Forget Mejia," Tony said. "He's just window dressing."

Aisha made a face. She pointed at Janiah. "No. Think about him. Why's he important? What's he guarding? What gets stolen? What gets all the local masters all hot and bothered?"

"The sword," Janiah sighed. Janiah brightened a bit. "Chanchai's a pretty well-known master." Janiah looked at Aisha. "Maybe 1488 was after him."

"Let it go, sis." Tony shook his head slowly from side to side. "We know that 1488 wasn't expecting Chanchai to show up down in the subway. He was looking for somebody else."

"Who was he expecting? Who fits?" Aisha asked simply.

"The intended victim should have some connection with the pattern," Janiah said. She was on her feet and walking restlessly around. Aisha and Tony remained quiet and simply watched her as she added up the pieces of the puzzle. Janiah tried not to, but there was no avoiding it.

"Divine Mathematics' little sister, REK, was found dead in Brooklyn, stabbed to death in a robbery by someone they never found, which is why Divine Mathematics left New York and moved here."

Janiah felt like she had been struck. But part of her still struggled against the realization. She looked from Tony to Aisha and back again. "There's got to be some other explanation," she said.

Tony began to say "Bullshit," again but Aisha

shushed him.

"He wouldn't keep something like this from me," Janiah sighed.

"Maybe, Janiah." Tony said. He sounded sad, as if he was giving someone bad news. Which, in a way, he was. "But maybe not."

Tony looked down and shuffled some papers around in a rare moment of delicacy. A photocopy of a handwritten note caught her eye.

"What's that?" Janiah said quickly.

"The note that 1488 left at Martial Masters.," Tony replied. "It says, 'Please meet me' and gives three map coordinates and another shorter number. We checked the coordinates and they lead to nowhere." Tony handed it to her.

Janiah took a deep breath and asked, "Who said these are map coordinates, Tony?" Janiah did not want to hear the answer.

"Divine Mathematics," Tony said. "Why?"

"These aren't map coordinates," Janiah said. "If we keep with the mathematics theme and look at the numbers at letters, it says—" She grabbed a pen and began to write furiously on a piece of scrap paper, pausing to count out the number equivalents to the letters on her fingers. Finally, she spoke again. "It says, 'I look forward to meeting you again.' And the shorter number is a signature; a name... 'Go Gao'."

Tony silently mouthed the name and wrote it down. Janiah stood there with the paper clutched in her hand and felt the heat rise in her face. "I can't believe it," Janiah finally said. "He knew... all along."

Tony and his wife sat and said nothing. After that, Janiah didn't either. They all knew where things were heading.

***

Black Fists and Afros was quiet. Tony was right next to Janiah. He still was not firing on all cylinders, but Janiah could feel the anticipation boiling up in him. She pushed the buzzer but got no answer. There had been no activities planned at the school since the attack on James. But as a senior student and Full Instructor, Janiah had a key, so she opened the door. It wasn't unusual. Divine Mathematics encouraged his students to train relentlessly. Class did not need to be in session.

Anger clouds perception. Janiah was not focusing on the dim, empty space of the training floor as she entered. She never even sensed the presence behind the door until the business end of a pistol was shoved in her face. The man holding it took a good look at them and relaxed. Janiah wished she could say the same.

Tony had gone very still. His eyes were narrowed down to slits and he looked at the man with the gun like he was imprinting him in his memory for later, because Janiah could tell that there would be a later.

The man was a thug. He had the look written all over him. A young man with dark brown skin and light brown eyes. His hair was cut short on the side and in a spiky afro on top, with red highlights. His pistol was polished black steel—a Glock 17 large frame 9mm.

He had relaxed slightly, but he never took his eyes off of Janiah and Tony. And the gun did not waiver.

"Visitor!" he called upstairs.

Two young men appeared at the landing above the training space.

"Please, Bobo," Janiah heard Divine Mathematics say, then his voice dropped to a whisper.

Another voice called out an order. The gun lowered. Janiah and Tony went upstairs.

Janiah had generated a real head of steam on her way down to the school, but the experience of having a gun shoved in her face knocked her off balance mentally. At any other time, she knew if she mentioned that to her teacher, he would nod and reply that emotion does that sort of thing. But Janiah was not in the mood for any of his mystical advice. She wanted answers to something much more pressing.

Even someone not as skilled as Divine Mathematics would have sensed the tension coming from the Macks. But part of Janiah was surprised at Tony's emotional control. At least one of them was calm.

Divine Mathematics could see it in Janiah's face: the anger, the hurt. She had labored long with him but she felt all her skill slipping away, melted down by emotion. He saw that in her face, but he said nothing. His expression was stone cold.

"My apologies, Ms. Mack," the man called Bobo said. "My assistant meant no disrespect."

Bobo was an older man, probably in his early sixties, but he had the thick, solid look of someone who was still formidable. He was impeccably dressed: dark blue suit, white shirt, and gleaming black shoes. His crimson tie reminded Janiah of the color of blood.

Tony drew his big revolver from his shoulder holster. "I don't know who you are, but you just made a big mistake," he said. He nodded at Bobo. "Call down and have your 'assistant' drop the piece. Then we'll talk."

Bobo grimaced. "Please, sir, I think there's been a misunderstanding."

Tony eyed everyone carefully, turned partially so the gun was shielded from sight from the man downstairs. "Oh, I think there's been a misunderstanding, all right," Tony said.

"Mack, please!" Divine Mathematics said.

Janiah ignored him for a second then said, "That guy down there is a thug. He doesn't belong here."

"Indeed," Divine Mathematics said, in a tone that told Janiah to take it no further. Bobo had presented Tony with a silver badge that managed to pacify him. Tony put his gun away.

"Please come in, Mack," Divine Mathematics said. "Since you're both here—" He gestured to the sitting area and glided in without a backward glance.

Janiah obeyed and followed him in, pulled into the wake of sheer power that radiated from him. It had a subduing effect. But she fought it. Tony's presence helped. Once in the sitting room, Tony drifted to a wall and leaned against it, keeping an eye on everyone and on the stairwell. Divine Mathematics began the process of formally introducing her to his guest.

Janiah shook Bobo's hand. Divine Mathematics had introduced him as a U. S. Army Criminal Investigations Special Agent but Janiah had no time for introductions. "Excuse me," Janiah said to Bobo. "I have business with

Divine Mathematics." Then she faced her teacher. She could feel her lips curving downward with sadness as she prepared to speak. He stood there, unblinking.

"Who is Go Gao?" Janiah asked.

"That doesn't concern you," Divine Mathematics said, his eyes narrowing.

Janiah heard Tony snort. "The police will have a different idea."

"Doesn't concern me!" Janiah blurted out. She took a step toward him.

Out of the corner of her eye, she saw Bobo's body shift as if he was preparing to move. She spotted a matching shift from her brother. "James was almost killed. My brother was down there, too." Janiah felt her stomach muscles clench with tension.

Divine Mathematics was unmoved. Bobo spoke: "Ms. Mack, please."

Janiah ignored him and glared at Divine Mathematics.

"This isn't for the Eighty-Fivers," Bobo hissed.

Bobo probably didn't think Janiah understood Five Percenter lingo. The look Janiah gave him told him otherwise. "Eighty-Fiver." Eighty-Five Percenter—Eighty-five percent of the world's population, described as "uncivilized people; poison animal eaters; slaves suffering from mental death and lack of power; people who did not know their origin in the world. Eighty-Fivers were easily led in the wrong direction, but hard to lead in the right direction. Inferior.

In that brief statement, Bobo had crystallized the situation. However long Janiah had labored with her teacher, she was still not accepted as a true disciple. Whatever the secret he harbored, she was still unworthy of learning it. She felt the bitter realization that all she had attempted to achieve with Divine Mathematics was an illusion. The community she believed she was forging in his school was an exercise in wishful thinking.

The night Janiah performed at Martial Masters, she had felt the undercurrent of those sentiments from the other masters there. But she had believed her teacher—a Black man; a man proud of his African heritage and a long-time member of the Five-Percent Nation—to be above that kind of narrow thinking. As the true situation hit her, she had a sensation of vertigo, a swirl of disorientation.

Divine Mathematics stood there, rooted to the ground and said nothing. He was like a boulder on a sandy shore; waves pounding against him but with no visible effect. His students admired this in him. A day ago, Janiah had, too. Now, she wanted to wring his neck. But even after all this, she couldn't.

She brought her face close to his. "You knew," Janiah hissed. "You knew and you said nothing." It was as close as she could come to an actual physical attack. The closeness, the emotion made her words like nothing Janiah had ever done to him. It was odd, in a place devoted to combat, that there was normally so little emotional contact.

"Divine Mathematics," Tony said quietly. He had stopped leaning against the wall. "I think you've got information related to these murders." His words came out dipped with anger. "You held out on us, and my partner's in a world of hurt. I'm gonna tell the police. They're gonna get a warrant. And I'm gonna be responsible for them bringing you in. And when they do, you're gonna be in a world of hurt, too."

"Teacher, please!" Janiah cried. "Whatever you know, you've got to tell us. I was down there. I saw what the killer did."

Janiah's words did not move the old man. Divine Mathematics did not even flinch.

"My brother was down there!" Janiah went on. "You owe it to me."

Even now, she hoped for something, some reaction. An acknowledgment of his complicity. But her teacher stayed mute and Janiah turned away. "My brother was down there," Janiah repeated quietly, as much to herself as to Divine Mathematics.

Janiah stormed down the stairs and through the school, then headed toward the street. Tony turned to follow, but first he gave the two men in the upper room a look that said he would be back. The thug looked up as they came down the stairs and their eyes met. But emotion had no place there. Divine Mathematics had taught her that much. When the anger burned through, all that was left was a type of pride.

Janiah left *Black Fists and Afros.*

CHAPTER FOURTEEN

There's a spot in Stone Mountain Park where, on any given weekend, hordes of kite flyers are there. The kites, ranging from simple to elaborate, are brightly colored, and they whip and twist in the breeze like living things. Even on a weekday morning, there were a few retirees, clutching lines and watching the kites intensely.

There were young mothers with strollers that paused, pointing out the spectacle of the kites to their children. The colors and motion, the bright blue of the day spoke of good times, leisure, and joy uncomplicated.

Janiah had sprinted around the mountain that morning, as hard as possible. It didn't help. In some ways, it showed just how confused she was: she ran in pursuit of the Way that Divine Mathematics had opened to her. Now, even though she was turning her back on it, the discipline would not release its hold. The tether had been forged over years and years. No matter how she tried to break free, the training still had mastery over her.

Janiah stood, sweaty in the breeze, and watched the kites swoop in vain attempts at liberation, buffeted by the wind.

The day was bright. She turned away from watching and sat on a bench. She closed her eyes and savored the deep, warm push of sunlight. After running, even on a bad day, there was a type of calm. Janiah knew it was just endorphins at work, but it was welcome anyway.

It was, of course, at times when people are most relaxed that the more subtle powers come into play. Divine Mathematics taught that ase is the invisible energy that filled the world. The ability to connect with ase was latent in all of us. And it flowered when our mental tensions dissipated. Ase was what martial artists were supposed to harness. But sometimes, our ase manifested in disturbing and unexpected ways, like the insights we are left with on waking after a bad dream.

The breeze played against her on the bench. Janiah could hear the distant rush of cars as they shot by on the nearby main road and odd fragments of voices from the kite flyers. She breathed deeply on the bench with her eyes closed and gradually felt a type of awareness wash over her.

She felt him there.

It wasn't a mental thing. It had a far more visceral feeling, almost like a low-level electric current was passing through her body. And, as the feeling came, she acknowledged a certainty so deeply that it failed to surprise her. Divine Mathematics was near.

Janiah remained perfectly still, eyes closed, and explored the experience. When she was ready, she opened her eyes.

He stood with his back to her. The wind pushed at his clothes, and the navy blue fabric danced around his body like smoke against an immovable pillar.

They looked at each other in silence. When he started to move toward her, Janiah stood up.

"The awareness done come for you," Divine Mathematics said. He had felt it, too. At any other time, Janiah would have been pleased at the comment. But she was still too hurt.

"Not bad for an Eighty-Fiver," Janiah said.

His jaws tightened with displeasure, but he gestured toward the bench. "Please."

Janiah eased back down. Divine Mathematics sat stiffly, as if bracing himself against an unseen force.

"I'm surprised they let you go," Janiah told him.

He looked off in the distance at the kite flyers. "I made a statement,' he said. "Bobo has... certain hookups. The district attorney seemed content. You gotta understand, Mack."

Janiah jumped in. "Oh, I understand, all right. Tony was right. You've been holding out on us."

"It ain't as simple as that."

"Oh, no," Janiah said. "Probably complicated by having to deal with all these Eighty-Fivers."

"Stop," he grunted, making a short chopping motion with his hand. "You're guessing at things you don't know anything about."

Janiah stared at him, sitting there and gazing off into the distance. He felt the look and his head swiveled slowly around to face her.

"I don't know about things because you haven't

trusted me enough to tell me," Janiah said. "Me! After all this time."

He blinked once and seemed on the verge of saying something, but movement came easier to him. He rose slowly and walked across the grass. Janiah followed, like a fighter pressing an advantage, exploiting a weakness. There was some sort of subtle projection going on. Maybe it was ase. Maybe Janiah was just fed up. But they both felt it.

Divine Mathematics grasped his hands. "It is not your place to question my motives, Mack," he said. "Have I ever held back in teaching you?" He knew the answer and continued. "No. I haven't. I've worked with you for years."

"And I deserve your trust," Janiah said. She was not going to let him wiggle out of it.

Divine Mathematics straightened up and regarded her. "I've trusted you with the most precious thing I have. The Way."

"Don't give me that," Janiah said, waving her hand in dismissal. "When I needed you the most, you held back. And I want to know why."

An odd expression came upon Divine Mathematics' face, as if he was seeing Janiah for the first time. "This has changed you, Mack."

Janiah shrugged. This was a favorite tactic of his, changing angles of attack. Janiah was not going to be suckered in.

"There are some things we regret learning," he cautioned.

"I need to know," Janiah said.

Divine Mathematics sauntered across the field to the walking path. speaking softly. Janiah followed to hear what he had to say.

"I remember when you first came to the school," he said. "You were so hungry for knowledge." The corners of his mouth stretched into a wry smile.

They walked along, an old man and a young woman, sharing memories in the sun.

Janiah could think back to the years she had spent searching with him: searching for release from the pressures of graduate school, for solace when her father died. For a sense of place and belonging.

"Sometimes, our desire for something can work against us," he said. Janiah started to reply but Divine Mathematics held up a hand. "I'm thinking of your early days, Mack," he went on. "There is a danger of people who work with their minds too much. It creates an imbalance. That imbalance is revealed in motion, of course."

Janiah remembered that he used to yell at her to stop moving her head, but she refused to say so.

"Yeah," Divine Mathematics said as if reading her mind. "When everything you do involves your Ori, you tend to involve it in everything that you do. You telegraph your movements through odd little jerks of the head."

"I stopped," Janiah said, leery of a walk down memory lane. Her tone conveyed the sentiment.

"Yeah. You have approached a place where thought and emotion are more equally at balance," Divine Mathematics said. "It shows in your technique."

Janiah said nothing.

"Part of what you sought with me was that balance," the old man said. "It was what drew you to *Black Fists and Afros.*"

"I thought I was pursuing my African roots," Janiah said. "The culture." The words felt bitter in her mouth.

Divine Mathematics stopped and peered at her. "And now you reject my teaching? And all your hard work? For what?"

Janiah stood there with her fists balled on her hips. She leaned close to him. "You know the reason."

"I know what you *think* the reason is, Mack," he said calmly.

"Don't play with me!"

Now he really smiled and it made her even angrier. "Mack, it's interesting that a woman so cerebral should now let her emotions run so strong he said" He cocked his head to look at her as he began to walk again. "But that, too, is part of what you sought, right?"

It's a hard thing to explain to an outsider. Studying an art with a teacher like Divine Mathematics was many things: a physical challenge, an act of will, and it was a process of creating links between yourself and others, of making connections between people that were so strong because they were forged in heat and discipline and hope and vulnerability.

As Janiah stood there in the sunlight, she squinted to see Divine Mathematics. The glare was intense, and he was hard to see with the sun at his back. She could still feel him, however. And the sense of connection Janiah felt was only partially eclipsed by anger. And fear that they were being driven apart.

Janiah swallowed. "I need to know why you held back."

Divine Mathematics reached out and touched her arm. It was an unusual gesture. "The reasons are... not simple."

Janiah snorted. "Things never are with you."

"That doesn't mean that they aren't true." He seemed to straighten a bit, as if shrugging off a weight with a sudden decision. "You're right, Mack. I will explain. But not here. You should come to the school."

"Why?"

Divine Mathematics began to walk away. "Because you're my student," he said.

Her resentment was strong, but ultimately the connection between them proved stronger. Janiah followed his car back to *Black Fists and Afros.*

The training hall was once again empty of activity. The thug with the gun was there. And so was his boss, Bobo Foley.

Their first meeting had been a brief and awkward one, so they reintroduced themselves. Bobo shook her hand and offered a business card, to her. Janiah gave the card a quick glance. It was simple and elegant. The card stock was a fine cream and the lettering was gold. It contained his name and contact numbers and the Georgia Bureau of Investigation seal.

"Bobo is assigned to the GBI," Divine Mathematics said. He is actually a Master Sergeant in the army's Criminal Investigations Division.

Janiah must have been a disappointment to them both, since she did not swoon. She had more pressing issues on her mind. She wished they would get to the point.

"What do you know about the GBI, Ms. Mack?" Bobo asked. His voice had a forceful, precise tone.

"It's a state law enforcement agency," Janiah replied as they sat down.

"Right, Bobo said. "Do you have any idea what the Criminal Investigations Division, or CID is?" It was a rhetorical question, and he went right on without waiting for her response. "The CID investigates felony crimes and serious violations of military law & the United States Code within the United States Army. The CID is a separate military investigative force with investigative autonomy."

"And the CID travels with thugs?"

"Ah," he said. "You're talking about the young man below us." Something like an ironic smile appeared on his face. "He is not GBI or CID. I'm here... unofficially. In light of events, I hired him as muscle."

"A hired gun?" Janiah said. "What's there to be afraid of?"

"In addition to more... mundane work," he eventually said as he studiously ignored her comment, "the CID has more specialized duties. We must remain alert to soldiers going rogue and harming civilians, especially highly trained, very dangerous special ops soldiers."

"And what does that have to do with my teacher, or the Five-Percenters?"

"The unit I head in CID is known as *God-Body*," The pace of his words was hesitant, as if he was mentally reviewing what could be divulged before speaking. Then the tempo picked up, as if he had made a decision. "We use special tactics in containment and neutralization of threats to national security." He sounded like he had that part memorized. Probably came from the mission statement.

"God-Body trainees receive extremely intensive training in several fighting systems. We also use the lingo of the Five-Percenters as a coded language. A soldier in God-Body must hold a high ranking in some martial arts, must pass a battery of tests with high scores and must be at least 50% of Black American heritage. We pay the most skilled martial arts masters in the world to train us. And the training never really ends."

Questions flickered through Janiah's mind in a steady stream. They were somehow treading on very sensitive ground. She could sense it from Bobo's body language and that of her teacher. She did not want to spook them with her directness, but little bells were going off in her head. Highly trained martial artists. Five-Percenter lingo. And a trail of bodies that stretched across the country. Janiah had to ask.

"Teacher, is there a connection between this Go Gao and the CID?"

Janiah looked from one face to the other. In the quiet of the room, she could hear traffic from far away. A car door slammed. Down below them, a man with a gun waited with the mute intensity of a raptor.

Bobo regarded her silently. The air quivered with tension. The two men exchanged looks. Bobo seemed angry at having to disclose things. Divine Mathematics seemed resigned.

"What does this have to do with the murders?"

Janiah asked. "Why is he here?"

"The answer is simple," Divine Mathematics finally said. "Go Gao is looking for me."

Which is all he said for a time.

The story Divine Mathematics eventually told unfolded with a hypnotic cadence that brought the images he evoked vividly to mind. The tale spun out in starts and stops, a line of events anchored in his past and pulled painfully into his present.

The elite corps of God-Body had tried to hire Divine Mathematics—who had just started making his name as the best unarmed and weapons fighter in the New York martial arts community—to teach them his skills. Divine Mathematics refused. "I don't teach the police, the military, or anybody else with a history of oppressing Black people," he said.

Bobo had assured him that every soldier in God-Body was Black and that their job was to neutralize rogue military personnel.

Divine Mathematics still refused, but agreed when his little sister, REK said she wanted to teach. Divine Mathematics attended the workshop with her for her safety.

Which is where he met Go Gao.

"Wait... Go Gao is Black?" Janiah said, shocked. "Chanchai said he was Asian."

"His father is Chinese and Go Gao looks like a Chinese man with a deep tan," Bobo said. "Go Gao's mother, a Black woman from Chicago, was an English teacher in Guangzhou, which is where she met his father. Go Gao was raised in Guangzhou until he was twelve, then he moved with his family to San Francisco."

"His daddy ran a Chow Gar Tong Long—Southern Praying Mantis—school in Guangzhou and later in San Francisco's Chinatown," Divine Mathematics chimed in. "Go Gao trained under his father from two years of age until his father died from cancer when he was sixteen."

"A year later, Go Gao's mother remarried—a brother who was a high-ranking student of Go Gao's father. That man, Booker Williams, took over the Gao Kwoon. Go Gao felt that he should have run the school, but his mother felt he was too young and immature. Upset, the young Gao enlisted in the army when he was eighteen and left San Francisco for good.

"I saw that Go Gao—he was only twenty-three or twenty-four back then—had within him the potential for greatness," Divine Mathematics said. "After my sister's workshop, he begged to train under me. But like I said, I don't teach the military or the police. Unknown to me, my sister had started dating Go Gao and they developed a serious relationship. She was teaching him on the sly, too."

As he described the events of twenty years ago, Janiah could see her teacher's pain.

"I didn't find out they had been dating until Go Gao suddenly went AWOL," Divine Mathematics said. He began rapidly tapping the floor with his foot. "After being missing for three days, the MPs went to his apartment looking for him. He was gone. But REK was in his bed... with fourteen stab wounds to her chest and an '8' carved on each cheek."

"Oh my God," Janiah gasped.

"Yeah," Divine Mathematics sighed. "She was his first victim."

"It's believed Go Gao had developed a hatred of Black people," Bobo said. "His mother marries a Black man just a year after his father dies; that same Black man then takes over his father's martial arts school instead of him; then Divine Mathematics rejects him as a student. I think that rejection was the final straw."

"And after all these years... after you knew I was involved with this case... you couldn't tell me?" Janiah asked, still upset with her teacher.

"I wanted you to give up the case," Divine Mathematics said. "I didn't want you in the sights of a man like Go Gao. You remind me so much of her."

"Of who?" Janiah asked. "Your sister?"

Divine Mathematics was quiet for a long while. Finally he spoke in a whisper, "Yes." A tear ran down his cheek.

At that moment, all Janiah's anger for her teacher left her. She had never seen him vulnerable. She did not know what to say, so she fought back tears of her own and changed the subject, "And it's taken him this long to locate you, Teacher?"

"I did not want to be found," Divine Mathematics said simply.

"What has happened is regrettable, Ms. Mack," Bobo interjected. "When your teacher left New York, he maintained contact with only a select few. It is only recently that we've been in contact." Bobo paused for a moment to let that sink in before he continued. "I had known for years that Go Gao would kill again. When I learned of the killings of the martial artists, I feared for Divine Mathematics."

Janiah thought of the hatred Go Gao must have

harbored. The emotional impact of such a rejection. From hurt to hate is a small step.

"Now," Bobo continued, "I believe that Go Gao's search is over."

Janiah looked at her teacher. "How can you be sure?"

Divine Mathematics smiled. "Go Gao hoped to deal with me the night your brother's friend was wounded. He stole Yasuke's sword to provoke me. We had a discussion about Black people historically in Asia and Yasuke was at the forefront of the conversation. I revealed that Yasuke is one of my inspirations for training. He left me clues that he had tracked me through Wulff... through Coutinho... he's here. Somewhere. He'll come for me again."

"I don't believe this," Janiah said.

"Please," Bobo said. "There's no doubt."

Janiah looked at Divine Mathematics: he merely closed his eyes and nodded in affirmation.

Bobo continued. "Everything else has been a prelude. The wild dog now hunts your master, Ms. Mack."

CHAPTER FIFTEEN

In the news room, phones chirped and papers rustled. Reporters called to one another over their cubicle separators. There was a low-level hum of activity, the air filled with the sound of people just barely keeping the influx of information under a semblance of control. Back on the job, Tony functioned with the easy efficiency of a man in his element.

He had taken in Divine Mathematics' statement without comment. He was silent when the D.A. let Janiah's teacher go. Now, Tony was cold, dispassionate, and efficient. His words were tight and fast, as if shaped by the effort of self-control, but he did not say a thing that revealed his anger. He was too focused on the information and its impact on the hunt for James' attacker.

The police and the press now had a name. A description. Something to narrow the odds. Motivation was less important now. Tony knew that Go Gao was in the city and why he had come. He had been a crime reporter long enough to know that you could torture yourself endlessly with trying to figure out why people did things. It was enough to know that they did them. At the very least, it kept him employed.

He had been invited by the police to join a conference in the Bat Cave, where the detectives mapped out a strategy for finding Go Gao. Janiah had not been invited, but her brother filled her in on the nuts and bolts of the manhunt. There were endless checks of hotels and motels; a review of airline manifests; questioning of Über and Lyft drivers; the citywide distribution of a description to all police precincts and media outlets.

"Sounds like y'all have it under control, Tony. What do you need me for?" Janiah asked.

He squinted at her. "I've got questions." He settled back in his desk chair and rummaged around for a cigarette. He pulled a bent one from his top drawer, looked at it longingly, then at the 'No Smoking' sign James had posted on the wall beside his desk. A handwritten addition scrawled across the bottom read: "This means you!" Tony sighed and dropped the cigarette back in the drawer.

"Chanchai says Go Gao used a sword that night in the subway."

"A katana." Janiah said. "But he doesn't do Japanese martial arts."

Tony nodded. "Okay, whatever," he said.

"No katana was used in the other two homicides," Janiah said.

"That tells me that Go Gao probably got the weapon after Coutinho was killed," he said. "I gotta assume that you don't get these things at *Dollar General*."

"There are places you can get them in Atlanta," Janiah said. "But if this thing is a real katana, and I have to believe it is, based on Chanchai's description and the wounds—" Janiah tapered off, and thought of James.

Tony gave her a come-on gesture. "Yeah, I know; I know. How many places can you buy a real sword like that around here?"

"Well, you can get cheesy knock-off versions of a samurai sword at military supply and martial arts supply stores all over town. But I don't think Go Gao would use something like that. Not for something as important as killing a martial arts master. There are probably two or three people who could sell you a real one in the A."

Tony tossed her a pad. "Names. Addresses. I'll pay' em a visit."

"It's not that easy, Tony," Janiah said. "Most swords like this are custom made. They have to be ordered way in advance. From Japan. You can check, but I doubt Go Gao was able to get something like this on short notice."

Janiah noticed the display catalogue from Martial Masters on a pile of papers. She never did get a chance to see the show. It seemed like something so distant it was unreal. Janiah picked the thing up. It was a glossy brochure that incorporated some of the stuff she had developed for Nemesio Pena. "You're talking about weapons like these, Tony," Janiah said, waving the catalogue at him.

"Okay, so where'd he get it?" Tony asked.

Janiah shrugged, and to stall while she thought, she leafed through the pages of Pena's show. She was turning a page when something caught her eye. For a minute she could not quite figure out what was bothering her. Then it became clear.

Tony had been fidgeting in impatience but grew still as he read her body language. "What?" he asked.

"This is weird," Janiah answered. "I had a chance to

look at photos of some of the display items when I was writing that piece for Pena. I remember this sword here—" Janiah pointed at it. "But the photo of the sword in the catalogue is different."

Tony looked at it with interest. "How so?"

"The handles are different shapes, Tony," Janiah said. "This sword is supposed to be four-hundred years old. An ancient Japanese sword's hilt is fluted toward the butt end. It helps you keep your grip on the sword so you don't drop it in combat. Modern swords tend to have a relatively straight hilt." Janiah looked up at her brother. "Somebody must have gotten the pictures mixed up. Because this sword is not the one I had written about."

"A sword like this is valuable?" Tony asked. Janiah nodded and he smiled. "And you could still use it to kill somebody?"

"Yeah."

"Well, sis, I think we've found where Go Gao got his weapon."

"Huh?"

"We know he was in the gallery the night he killed Mejia. After you saw the picture of the sword. But before the catalogue was printed. He had opportunity. And a motive."

"But no katana was reported missing," Janiah said. Just the bokken." "You'd think Pena would want to make an insurance claim."

Tony got a crafty look on his face. "You know, all this karate-kung fu stuff has really made this whole case hard to figure out," he said. "Everything is way too exotic for me.

But this... this kinda thing I get. Maybe Pena didn't want any more adverse publicity. Maybe he didn't want to scare away backers... Maybe, just maybe, his insurance coverage is shady."

"But he had to get all kinds of insurance for his show. He told me. Said it was costing a fortune."

Tony sat back and made some quick notes. "Precisely," he said. "And if you had to come up with a name of someone who might be likely to cut corners, who would you suggest?"

Janiah got the point. "Nemesio Pena."

Tony jumped up. "Okay, I'm outta here. Got enough to work on for now."

"What about me?"

He shrugged into his coat. "You've helped enough. Take off. Go... I don't know. Go do what you do."

So Janiah did.

***

The tiny waterfall in Divine Mathematics' garden flows over gray rocks. It makes a musical sound that fills the small, green space behind Black Fists and Afros. Divine Mathematics tends the yard with a remorseless intensity. It is (nonetheless) green and soothing in the summer and, like the man himself, the product of discipline and a fierce attention to details. In the garden grows tomatoes, watermelons and collard greens—Divine Mathematics' favorite foods.

Janiah and her teacher sat on the little covered porch overlooking rocks and shrubs, watching small birds bounce and flutter in the yard's stillness. Divine Mathematics talked quietly and evenly, his voice an expression of the garden's mood. An outsider would never guess he was talking with her about the finer points of killing a man.

When Janiah had arrived earlier, the training hall had been silent. There was still tension between them, and Divine Mathematics and Janiah had drifted down into the empty training hall, instinctively seeking comfort in the familiarity. The afternoon sun slanted in and cast bright stripes on the navy blue arms of Divine Mathematics' bowling shirt. He stood alone in the center of the room, holding a wooden machete in a low defensive posture. His eyes seemed focused on something far away, but as Janiah joined him, the sword swung up to track her. Janiah had told him what the police and the press were doing. He did not seem particularly surprised at the turn of events. But the awareness of Go Gao's intentions seemed to be still sinking in.

"So, I suppose this is inevitable," he said. "The past cannot be avoided."

"That would be too simple," Janiah said.

"Too simple?" Divine Mathematics said with a smirk. "Naw. I think it's too complicated."

Janiah looked quizzically at him.

He sighed as he gathered his thoughts. "Mack, to create a warrior of this skill level is a work of many years. It requires great care. Attention's gotta be paid, not only to technique but to the trainee. Their spirit becomes intertwined with their skills. If you take one away, the other suffers. Now we see the results."

Janiah said nothing.

"I doubt that God-Body had the patience to train correctly," her teacher continued. "They're the army, after all—their zeal is always greater than their wisdom."

Divine Mathematics glided smoothly across the floor. He placed the training machete in a rack on the wall and turned to face me.

"Go Gao will not cease until he gets what he desires," he said. "He will continue to... hurt others, especially those connected with me. I see that now." He looked directly at her, his night-dark eyes still and hard. "I ain't gon' let him destroy what I've built here."

"*Black Fists and Afros?*"

His head swiveled on his thick neck. "He's gon' strike at what I value most, Mack. My students... you."

Janiah felt an electric surge of panic. Her face flushed. But she controlled her breathing, and gradually her heartbeat began to slow again. She thought of the destruction Go Gao had left, deep and shocking. And now Divine Mathematics was certain there would be more. Janiah needed to think of a way to stop it.

It finally came to her. "Why not lay a trap?" she suggested. "We knew Go Gao's patterns and what he's after. Why not provide him with the victim?"

"So, I'll be the bait," Divine Mathematics said with a smirk.

Janiah nodded. They knew the killer was close, biding his time. He was a predator, slowly circling in the shadows, just out of sight.

"Go Gao needs to be attracted, Janiah said. "Not just tracked. We'll entice him to come to us. The hunt will become a seduction, made alluring by the scent of blood."

"Makes sense, Mack," Divine Mathematics said, nodding his head. "The trick is being bait that survives."

Divine Mathematics agreed to be the bait almost eagerly. There was, after all, avenging his sister involved. But he was skeptical about Janiah's assurances of safety, despite the fact that she thought that Tony and his connections on the police force would back them up.

"All bait gets eaten if the trap fails," Divine Mathematics said. "So can the hunters."

As a result, he treated his and Janiah's roles in the plan as if either of them might have to fight Go Gao. "It's what he wants, Mack," the teacher said.

And so he had exacted a price from her: he made her practice with him as he prepared for what he thought of as the inevitable confrontation with Go Gao. "It will add some variety to your training," Divine Mathematics said.

It had only been a few hours since that statement, and, as they sat there on the porch, Janiah was sore in all the ways familiar to her from her years of martial arts training. The only difference was that now she hurt everywhere all at once. The tiny muscles in her feet ached. Her stomach muscles spasmed involuntarily in certain positions. And she was tired.

"He hunts at night," Divine Mathematics said. "He uses the body's biorhythms as a weapon. The murders occur in the dark, when our ase, our vital energy, is ebbing."

Janiah thought about the murders. All nocturnal.

Most happened well after midnight. The quiet time, the hours when infants awake for comfort, when sleep cycles shift. The time when the old and the ill and the weak let life slip away.

"We'll need to work on rhythms, Mack," Divine Mathematics said. "You'll need to be here all through the training." It was a statement, not a question. The link between master and student was too strong for doubt. In some ways, it was a return to the balance of their former relationship. Divine Mathematics sat comfortably, a navy blue bowling shirt stretched over his thick torso, matching cargo pants covering his lower half and blue leather Converse All-Stars with black toe-caps covering his feet. He squinted out into the garden.

Janiah moved gingerly, and Divine Mathematics looked at her. "Are you tired?" he asked. "You gon' be. We'll work more on your meditation. It'll help with the fatigue."

Divine Mathematics had a hard time getting out of the role of instructor. Even though the training was really for him, he insisted on talking like it was something he was doing for Janiah. She had ceased to notice it and just nodded wearily in resignation.

"Physically, there's little room for improvement. But your skills—" he paused as if internally rating er abilities. He smiled. Small sparrows sputtered in the waterfall's pond, scattering droplets of water in a fine spray. "You're a good student, Mack. Among my best. At each step, you've struggled, but you keep on keepin' on. I like that."

Janiah was not sure what Divine Mathematics liked more about her: the fact that she had to struggle or the fact that she eventually learned much of what he taught her. It was typical of him. With Divine Mathematics, grading, like everything else, was a bit different from that of other arts.

Japanese, Korean and some Chinese martial arts stylists talked about rank and belts and promotion. Divine Mathematics used the African Way—at *Black Fists and Afros*, they did not wear belts, except to hold up their pants.

At *Black Fists and Afros*, there were only four different stages—student, Assistant Instructor, Full Instructor and Master. Each level was an acknowledgment that you could do some things and are ready to learn some more. A promotion to a different stage did not signal an end to training; there was no such thing. There was only the invitation to learn more.

So when Divine Mathematics paused and smiled, Janiah was sure he was mentally listing her faults and reliving her past struggles, all as a preparation for judging whether she could follow him further.

"This is gon' be hard for you, I think." He emerged from his interior reflection and focused on her. The sounds of the world outside were muted and far away. As he spoke, they faded further, or his words swelled despite their quiet tone, so that all Janiah could focus on was his teaching.

"It requires a total focus on the struggle," he said. "An absence of compassion. I've watched you for years. You're a good woman. This type of concentration and ruthlessness is hard for you. But it would be hard for any of us. But very necessary."

Janiah nodded.

"The evil to be faced... is powerful," he said. "It'll be relentless. All your wits, your skills will be needed to defeat this anjonu—*demon*. All that your body can bear."

Divine Mathematics stood up and began shuffling

and shifting around in a tight circle. "But there's more to learn."

He began brushing his shoulders downward rhythmically. "The spirit's gotta be focused. There can't be the least gap in concentration."

He tapped the sides of his forehead as he dipped and shuffled forward. "The luxury of mercy doesn't exist. Or fear. Or doubt."

Janiah had seen her teacher do this many times before—the wise words combined with the hypnotic, fluid movements. The breath control. He was summoning power, forging a link between body and spirit.

He started the movements again. Janiah leapt to her feet and flowed in imitation of her teacher. The rhythm of their minds moved in time with each breath. Their hands brought forth power from the earth and the air.

After a few minutes, Divine Mathematics walked over to a large iron pot against a corner of the school facing the garden: his shrine to Ogun—the Spirit of War. Around the pot were several pistols, rifles, bottles of beer, gin and vodka and a half-gallon jug of crimson palm oil. Inside the pot was an assortment of knives with the points jutting up out of it. He picked up a bottle of gin and then beckoned Janiah to approach him.

His voice seemed to come from deep inside him, from a place impossibly remote.

"Ògún O Ògún, onírè, oko ò mi. Irúnmolè tí ń rù mìnìmìnì. Òlómi nílé fèjè wè. Òlása nílé fìmobímo bora. Ògún aládàá méjì. Ó fikán sánko, ó fikán yènà. Ojó Ògún ń fikòlé òrun bò wá s'ílé ayé. Asa iná ló mú bora èwù èjè ló wo sorùn o. Ògún onílé owó olonà ola. Ògún onílé kángun kàngun òde òrun. Méje l'Ògún mi Ògún alárá nií gbajá. Ògún onírè a gbàgbò. Ògún ikolà a gbà 'gbín. Ògún elémoná nií gbèsun asu. Ògún akirun á gbà wo àgbò. Ògún gbénàgbénà eran ahun nií je. Ògún mákinde ti d'Ògún léhìn odi. Bí ò bá gba tápà á gbàbókí á gba húnkùnhúnkùn á gba tèmbèrí o jàre mo ní e má bógúnrún fijà sere. Ògún òlódodo l'Ògún tèmi. Omo Orórínà, omo Tàbúfú. Morú nítorípé l'ójó. Ògún kó délé ayé, Emu ló kó bèrè o mgbà tó délè irè o. Ògún onílé owó, Olónà olà Ògún onílé, kángun kàngun òde òrun. Mo ní e má aàbógùn fijà sére o o. Ara Ògún kan gó gó gó."

Divine Mathematics was testing her memory of the praise poem to Ogun. She translated: "Ogun Oh! Ogun, God of Iron, my protector," she began. "A deity that strikes heavily. He has water at home, but bathes with blood. He has clothes, but wears palm fronds. Ogun possesses two cutlasses: one for cutting grass, the other for making marks. Since Ogun came down from heaven to earth, he uses robes of fire as his cover, a shirt of blood is what he puts on. Ogun has a house of riches, a house of wealth. Ogun has a house of war in the Great Beyond. My God of Iron is seven. Worshippers of Ogun bring him a dog. Ogun also accepts a ram as sacrifice. The Ikola offer Ogun snails. The Elemona offer Ogun roasted yam. The brave bring Ogun a ram. The carpenter offers Ogun tree sap. Makinde, Ogun has become. If he sells Tapa, he will sell to his friend and he will collect three. Do not use the sword to play with the God of Iron. My Ogun is a truthful deity. The son of Ororina, so of Tabafu. I tell you because, when Ogun came into this world, he asked first for palm wine when he got to Ire. Ogun's house is full of money. His pathway is full of wealth. The owner of the ugly house in heaven. I tell you, do not fight playfully with Ogun. Ogun is not smiling at all."

"Thus we invoke you, Baba Irin... Father of Iron... to ask for strength, compassion, fearlessness. This you have promised to give to your warriors—the Dogs of Ogun. Here we kneel before you."

Divine Mathematics drank from the bottle of gin until his cheeks were round and full with alcohol, then he sprayed the Ogun shrine three times, forcing the gin from between his lips in a fine mist. Janiah followed suit. A moment later, she felt power rise in her. Starting at the soles of her feet and coursing up her spine. Ogun had come.

***

"How's James?" Janiah asked Tony wearily. She could hear the surge of her blood in the cell phone.

"The same," he said. "Hanging on."

"That's something, at least," she said. Tony grunted. "Any new leads?"

"We're working on it," Tony replied. "I shook your pal Pena's tree a bit."

"Anything fall out of it?"

Janiah could see the shrug, even over the phone.

"Something stinks there, but I don't have anything solid," he said. Then he switched gears. "What are you up to? I've been trying to reach you."

"I know," Janiah said. "Sorry. I got involved with something with Divine Mathematics." She tried to sound sincere, but it was an effort holding a conversation. Divine Mathematics had worked her ruthlessly for the rest of the day. She was sitting in one of the chairs in her teacher's living room upstairs. It was a comfortable seat. And it was good to talk. But some of the small muscles in her left hand were spasming. She could see them jump in the lamplight. Her brain felt pulled in two directions.

Janiah had not told Tony about her scheme yet. She wanted to ease him into it. So she let him know that Divine Mathematics wanted her to do some special intensive training with him. But that was all.

"It'll be a few days," she said evasively.

"Sometimes, Janiah, I don't get you at all," Tony sighed. "Okay, I might need to reach you there. Give me the number."

The muscles in her right calf, near the Achilles tendon, were starting to tighten up. Janiah felt like she had tightly strung cables in her legs and was trying to ignore it and listen hard to the inflections in her brother's voice. He knew something was up.

Janiah gave him the number, said good-bye, and sat there with her eyes closed. *Idiot*, she thought. *You should have told him. He's had enough of people holding out on him.*

"Your conversation was upsetting." Her eyes snapped open. Divine Mathematics had slipped into the room and sat across from her. His face was impassive, but his eyes were alive.

Janiah exhaled slowly and nodded.

"Your brother doesn't understand what's going on?"

"Nope," Janiah said, shaking her head.

"Mack, listen to me," Divine Mathematics said. "You're wise not to involve him. A sphere of danger surrounds us here. If you bring people close to you, they'll be in a world of trouble. It's obvious you care for your brother. And you're wise not to inform him of your plans. If you can shield him, you gotta do so. Even if it means that he'll be upset."

Janiah sighed. "I know, Teacher, but—"

He held up a hand, palm out. Divine Mathematics' hands looked like the rest of him—hard, fierce and capable. Even his words of comfort had a brutal tinge to them. "But nothing, Mack," he said. "Which is better, that your brother feels hurt for a time because he doesn't fully understand your motives, or that you gush out your secrets and he runs to your side, endangering his life? He's already suffered enough."

Janiah nodded.

"If you pull him close at this moment, you'll place him within the dark circle. He is, I'm sure, a good journalist. But he's got no place here."

Divine Mathematics looked up and gazed out the window. Lights fought the darkness, cutting at it, beating it back in spots, but ultimately, the brightness bled away, surrendering to the infinite strength of the night. The teacher's eyes were unfocused, as if he was intent on something beyond mere sight. For a moment, in the lamplight, Janiah could see the toll of years on him. Maybe, in his own way, he was trying to explain why he had kept things from her for so long.

"Make no mistake, Mack," the old man went on. "Go Gao is coming. I can feel it."

***

In the night, Janiah slept fitfully. Outside Divine Mathematics' school, cars rumbled by, radios pounding. Distant horns sounded. Sirens shrieked and died away.

Janiah drifted into a drowsy half-sleep. Her body jerked involuntarily as muscle tension began to dissipate. Divine Mathematics startled her when he woke her.

"Get up, Mack. It's two-thirty."

Janiah stood and focused on his stolid silhouette beside her in the dark.

"Time to train," he said.

CHAPTER SIXTEEN

The heavy fire door boomed open, echoing in the empty school. Divine Mathematics and Janiah had rested at dawn, and Bobo and his hired help had arrived shortly afterward. The two senior men conferred quietly, while the thug waited in the shadows. The first floor practice room was empty of students, but Bobo's watchdog scanned the empty air.

Bobo had a reserved face that gave you the illusion of total control. But he was not as cool as he pretended to be: he looked up sharply at the sound when the door banged.

Janiah went to see who it was. It was one of those automatic things you do for your teacher. Before she could even get to the foot of the stairs, however, the thug had jumped in front of her. He drew his pistol from under his shirt, like a magician pulling a bouquet out of the air with a simple flourish.

The thug glided across the floor ahead of Janiah, the gun's muzzle cutting through the space.

Divine Mathematics followed them down the stairs but said nothing, watching the action with professional dispassion.

The intruder stood with hands on his hips and regarded the thug. He looked at me, then back at the man with the gun, and clearly felt the need to defuse the situation.

"Take it easy, homeboy," he said. "I'm one of the good guys, remember?"

Janiah's brother had come to visit.

Looking at him, Janiah could tell he had been through a hard few days. But she was glad he had come. When Tony pushed open that door, he let in street sounds, heat, and the almost palpable tug of memory. All the drills and lectures and prayers to Ogun had begun to make her feel like a woman in suspended animation. They may have been setting a trap, but she was the one who felt imprisoned, set off from the real world. Tony restored her sense of connection. Janiah could guess that Divine Mathematics thought her brother's presence was bad for the training he was trying to accomplish. She, however, grinned like an idiot.

Tony stood there, dressed in old running shoes, even older khaki pants, and a dark blue t-shirt with a little *Fox-5* news show logo on the breast. He looked at Bobo's hired gun with a placid expression, gingerly holding his hands out at his sides to show he had no weapon.

"Hey, come on," Janiah said. "We've been through this before."

Eventually, the thug relaxed, although he looked annoyed that he had not been able to shoot anyone. Tony glared at him silently as he came upstairs, and said hello to Divine Mathematics. It wasn't a warm greeting. Janiah held her breath. Tony had a long memory and a short temper. From his perspective, Divine Mathematics was partly to blame for this mess and he felt there were still things he was not being told. He was right, of course, but now Janiah was the one holding out on him.

Bobo did not say much when Tony showed up. The two men eyed each other warily, but Tony did not even acknowledge him. Instead, he looked at Divine Mathematics and said, "I came to take my sister off your hands for a while."

Divine Mathematics looked at Janiah then turned to her brother and nodded. "She's been behaving. Enjoy the afternoon." Divine Mathematics gestured toward the street.

***

They drove down Cascade until it turned into Ralph David Abernathy and then toward West End Park on Oak Street. Both sets of grandparents had lived around there, and they had spent a lot of childhood Sundays visiting the area, watching relatives decay and the neighborhoods change. West End Park was different from the park of their childhood, but it certainly was lively.

Muslim women, covered from head-to-toe, including their faces, were wandering in and out of local stores and restaurants. Racks of Kente cloth dresses and t-shirts extolling the coolness, excellence and greatness of being Black were on display on the sidewalks. Even though they had the car windows closed and the AC on, Janiah could hear the Djembe music played by the drummers in the park.

"How you doing, Tony?" Janiah asked. His face had a tired, drawn look, but his eyes were clear.

"I'm okay. You, on the other hand, look like hell."

Janiah had not paid attention to a mirror in a while,

but she imagined that all the training with Divine Mathematics showed. She stayed silent and let him drive. There was a point to the visit, and Tony would get to it when he was ready.

"Hey, look," Tony said. "SUCC."

The parish of Sankofa United Church of Christ was marked by a large church complex looming over one whole block. The school building was tucked away in the back. Tony parked in the driveway entrance to the school parking lot. The entrance gate to the lot was chained shut and the building was dark and silent. Tony placed James' police sticker in the window then hopped out of the car and walked away without a second thought. It was one of the cool things about having a best friend who is a police officer, Janiah figured: ordinary parking rules don't apply. *Now if they'd stop murdering us and arresting us just for being Black, it'd be even cooler*, she thought.

The church was a huge brick building with large entrance doors that faced the avenue. The cavernous main hall of the church was dark and locked, but the smaller lower-level was open. Janiah's family had been baptized, gotten married in, and buried their father in this church, and it was familiar ground for both of them. As children, they had spent what felt like an eternity at a host of services there. Being there did not do much for Janiah's and Tony's piety, but it did create their immense capacity for tolerating boredom. They also developed the ability to sit very quietly for long periods of time.

Tony went in, and Janiah followed. Working with Divine Mathematics had put her in a heightened state of suspicion and sensitivity. Janiah did not think it was likely Go Gao would be anywhere near at this time of day, and he certainly would not be interested in her. But, as her teacher kept drilling into her head, awareness was the key to survival. Janiah took a hard look around.

The ceiling in the lower church was not very high, nothing like the soaring vaults one story up, and the view of the altar was blocked by the pillars that supported the floor of the church above. It broke up their line of sight, and the feeling was that almost anyone could be lurking there. *Maybe even God*, Janiah thought, scanning the room. An old man slowly shuffled down the center aisle toward the doors. To their right, a woman knelt, obscured in a kerchief and dark blue raincoat. Her eyes were red-rimmed and moist. Her lips were dry and worked in a constant, mumbled litany. Beads on her neck made faint clicking noises. It was the sad cast of characters you find in any church in the daytime.

The room smelled of wax and a hint of sage. The pews were old and dark, polished by the friction caused by years of ample backsides. Statues of African warriors and Black Jesus lined the walls, and banks of candles flickered in front of them.

Tony sauntered into the church. Janiah followed him to one of the side pews where a statue, dark with age, was located.

Tony stood staring at the statue for a while then he turned and went outside without saying a word.

They walked slowly around the perimeter of the church. The sidewalk was wide, and there were young trees planted in large squares of earth at regular intervals. The trees did not do much to cut the sun's glare.

"Do you remember Daddy telling us about these trees?" Tony asked. "Well, not these trees, exactly. These are replacements. But the originals?"

"Nope," Janiah said. "Not at all."

"There was some retired army dude who started a marching band in the church," Tony went on. "I forget his name. Well, he retired from like twenty years in the army and comes back to the church. He gets this marching band going. Uniforms and music—fifty, maybe a hundred boys. The pride of the church. Then the Gulf War breaks out. The guy pulls some strings and gets back on active duty, and organizes a volunteer brigade—all those boys who grew up marching to his orders and trusting him."

It was hot and the light color of the sidewalk threw up a glare. It was hard to see Tony's expression very well.

"So, off they go to Pakistan. They get a huge send-off here. Flowers and speeches. The pride of the area, all those children, all dressed up and eager to go. Most never came back, Janiah. They were used to marching band shit—moving in step, colorful uniforms, doing covers of Earth, Wind and Fire songs. They got over there and what they got was machine guns, tanks, artillery barrages and 'friendly' fire from the white American soldiers. They were churned into dust. The church never forgave the band leader for taking their children off to war. There's a tree planted here for each boy lost."

"That's some story, Tony," Janiah said. They had walked back to the car and now stood facing each other across the hood.

"Yeah, but do you get the point?" He asked. They got into the car and sat there in the stuffy quiet. Tony stared out the windshield for a minute, then turned to her.

"Look, Janiah. You're different, all right? Even as a kid. You've always been interested in weird shit. Mama and Daddy knew it. And you were stubborn."

"I still am," Janiah said, smiling. It did not make a dent in Tony's seriousness.

"You, always have to do things your way," Tony went on. "On your terms. Look at culinary school instead of Business school at Howard. Divine Mathematics. Foregoing a job as a chef with a regular check and insurance for a cooking show."

Janiah remained silent, waiting to see where he was going.

"But the point is, this is different," he said looking at her. The police are searching for Go Gao right now. It's just a matter of time before they catch him."

Janiah stayed silent.

"I know what you're up to," he said. "You think you're gonna trap him."

He said it with such finality that Janiah knew there was no dodging the accusation.

"We've got a good chance," she said.

"No," he said, expressionless. "Listen to me. For once in your life, listen." He was angry, but it was not his usual loud anger. He was was quiet and white hot, and his voice was focused and sharp.

"You can't deal with this on your terms. This is not some goddamn game or contest. This dude is a killing machine. He kills because he can. Because he wants to; maybe needs to."

The air in the car was stifling.

Tony paused a minute as if he was trying to contain

himself. "Look at the trees out there," he began again. "Every one of those children thought he was going out to fight on his terms. Some romantic battle. Good versus evil. Most never even came back in boxes. They're bits of bone that got swept up in a goddamn sand storm. You think all this martial arts stuff is gonna help you stop this dude. It's not."

Janiah protested. She told Tony that the idea was to entice Go Gao into a trap where they could deal with him. "Besides, even if all else fails, there's Divine Mathematics," she explained.

Tony started the car and the air conditioning began to wash some cool air over them. It seemed to leech some of the tension from the atmosphere as well.

"Janiah, this martial arts stuff... it's a hobby," he said. "You're good at it, but it's a hobby. A sport."

"It's more than that, Tony," Janiah said quietly.

"How many people have you killed, Janiah?"

Janiah remained silent.

"Go Gao has killed three we know of," Tony said. "He tried to kill my partner."

The light changed and they rolled on. Tony stared straight ahead. "I don't want you being number four."

They were quiet for a time. The familiar rhythm of driving acted like a tranquilizer: the whoosh of the air conditioner, the faint bumping of the tires as they hit seams in the road, the syncopated click of the turning signal. They watched the other cars and other people as if their presence was a guarantee of normality.

Finally, Tony asked, "Okay, what's the plan? How do we do this?"

"We?" Janiah said.

"We. You think I'm showing up at Mama's with the bad news that some lunatic killed you?" He smiled a little at the thought of it.

So Janiah gave him the briefing. Most of it, he knew. The pattern of Go Gao's attacks was at night or early morning in secluded places where the ritual duel could take place. Janiah did not dwell too much on Divine Mathematics' past and Go Gao's connection to God-Body. At this stage of things, it was just so much background noise.

"With Divine Mathematics as bait, we should be able to catch him," Janiah said.

"So you're not gonna kill him?"

"I'd like to," Janiah said. Then, she said, "Nah. We just need to stop him. Get him off the streets." She wasn't sure deep down about how truthful she was being, but she wanted to allay Tony's concerns. "You said it yourself," she added. "I've never killed anybody."

Tony pulled the car over and turned once more to look at his sister directly. "Cool, but there's another thing, Janiah. Why do you think Bobo is involved here?"

"Because he wanted to warn Divine Mathematics. And to catch the army's rogue soldier, Go Gao—a rogue soldier trained to catch other rogue soldiers. He's gotta do it before the army finds out and they maybe disband God-Body. I think we have a good chance."

"Fair enough," Tony said. "But let me remind you—

he's government. The government doesn't give a damn about warning what they consider to be collateral damage. There's gotta be more to it."

"Okay," Janiah said, not really seeing the point.

"Okay," he said, mimicking her. "So tell me, genius... how does this situation benefit Bobo?"

"He gets to catch Go Gao," Janiah answered.

"You mean arrest him?"

"Sure," Janiah replied with a shrug.

"These guys are from the same military special ops unit and Bobo's gonna bust this killer? In Atlanta? My news station, and every other one in the world, would be all over it."

"What do you mean, Tony?"

"I mean the last thing Bobo wants is to bust this guy. It would attract too much attention."

"So what's he after?"

"Bobo isn't working for the GBI and he's not doing this without the army's permission. They sent him here... to do things quietly and if it goes bad, the GBI takes the hit." He paused to let it sink in. "Bobo isn't here just to catch Go Gao, Janiah. He's here to make sure no one finds out about him."

"And?"

"And he wants to kill him. That's why he brought that fool with the spiky hair. He's not a thug; that's his cover. He's an assassin. Probably a Marine or CIA sniper. They're gonna stake Divine Mathematics out, and when their man gets into the kill zone, they're gonna open take him out and maybe Divine Mathematics, too."

He pulled back out into traffic and let her digest that for a while.

"So what do you think?" he asked.

"Makes sense," Janiah replied. "There's only one problem—"

"What's that?"

"Divine Mathematics has his own plan. And he's better than they think," Janiah said. She turned to look at her brother. "He's even better than *you* think, Tony. And so am I."

He looked into her eyes, studying her. Finally, he spoke. "Let's hope so."

He said it like he did not have much hope. They rode in silence for a few blocks and he continued. "Of course, Bobo and his goon also have another big problem."

"What?" Janiah was preoccupied thinking about the new angles Tony had presented.

"Now I'm on their case."

They pulled up in front of *Black Fists and Afros*. Tony parked the car.

"That's true, Tony," Janiah said. "You are the biggest pain in the ass I know."

He smiled ruefully. "All part of the love I got for you, sis."

"What?" she said, feigning shock. "You actually

admitted you love me?"

"Don't get used to it."

***

Tony half-saying he loved her actually made Janiah feel good. She didn't think he had ever said so. But the new angles about Bobo, about the thug, about Bobo's real plans for Go Gao... they bothered her for the rest of the day.

When Divine Mathematics had finished with some late-day training, Janiah asked him what would happen if things fell through. She did not ask Divine Mathematics whether he could deal with it. It would be insulting. But, as Tony had laid things out that afternoon, a sudden, troubling series of thoughts hit her: *What's the worst-case scenario? What if the trap doesn't work? If Tony misses? If Divine Mathematics fails? What if I have to face Go Gao?*

She asked her teacher the last question in her mind. He sat there and stared at her expressionless.

"You're capable of more than you think," he finally said. Whether you're *ready* is another question. I can't tell. Let's hope we don't have to find out."

CHAPTER SEVENTEEN

As the light began to fade, the assassin in Bobo's employ started getting more focused. The untrained would have started to fidget with tension. The young man just seemed to grow more still, absolutely immobile with the effort of waiting. Divine Mathematics looked at him and nodded with reluctant appreciation. Go Gao's pattern was to strike late at night, when the energy and focus of his victims were at their lowest. But Go Gao was also unpredictable. He had succeeded in besting the highly skilled before; no one wanted to take chances. They sat quietly. Moved slowly and carefully. Only their eyes shifted quickly.

If the assassin was like a predator hunkered down in the tall grass, his employer seemed more like a tightly wound spring. Whatever his relationship was to her teacher in the past, Janiah thought that it paled in comparison to his driving need to neutralize Go Gao. Deep down, Janiah imagined he looked at Divine Mathematics and herself as a secondary concern. They were, in the final analysis, just bait; expendable.

When Tony came back with her and parked herself in a chair, Bobo started to protest. Tony gave him a wicked smile.

Divine Mathematics looked at Janiah. "Is this what you want, Mack?"

Janiah nodded.

Divine Mathematics looked toward Bobo and said, "This man is a guest." It seemed to settle the issue. But Tony's presence clearly did not sit well with Bobo. It was one more element he did not have complete control over.

Divine Mathematics spent the evening talking with Janiah about the way a challenger went about confronting someone in a martial arts school.

"When I was a young man living in Brooklyn, challenge matches between students in different schools happened pretty often," he said. "Heads thought they were in Ancient China or some foolishness."

They were seated in the garden again. Somewhere in the building, Bobo and his assassin were staking out fields of fire and having hushed conversations.

"What were they like, Teacher?" Janiah asked.

After a few seconds' consideration, he replied, "They were... informative." His hands stirred slightly in his lap. "You could learn a lot from the experience."

I bet, Janiah thought.

"Of course, a lot of people were seriously injured or killed. That... and the deaths... were why New York outlawed them."

"How many of those challenges did you make, Teacher?" Janiah asked.

"None," he replied. "But I accepted more than I would

have liked."

"And you won them all?"

Divine Mathematics gave her a side-eye.

Janiah chuckled. "Of course, you did."

"In the old days, most of these young bucks would learn all their sensei, sifu or sabumnim could teach and then seek out 'instruction' at another school. A truly skilled fighter would go from school to school, challenging the best students and even the masters.

"The challenge needs to be done a certain way," Divine Mathematics continued. "The challenger tells the name of his school, his teacher and his lineage then he or she asks to 'compare'. Depending on the situation, the teacher might select a student to fight for him." He looked directly at Janiah. "I don't think this will suit Go Gao in this case, though."

Thank God, Janiah thought. But she tried not to let the relief show on her face. She had thought a great deal about the prospect of fighting. She knew someone had to do it and she wanted Go Gao stopped and punished. She wanted him destroyed for what he had done to James. But after all the years she had spent with Divine Mathematics, she knew, when push came to shove, that there was a chance she was not good enough to face Go Gao and prevail. It hurt her to admit it, but it was true. The slightest flaw in her performance would be fatal and meant that Go Gao could escape. This, Janiah rationalized, could not be allowed to happen.

But late at night, in the brief period of rest before her teacher summoned her for training in the darkness, the hot spark of her anger and resolve had been smothered by something dense and ominous. It was the thing all warriors struggle against every time a fight beckons. No matter who stands before you, it lurks there, too. They try not to name it, for words make the intangible more potent. But the thing that lurks there, cold and thick and lifeless as mud, is fear.

Divine Mathematics was looking at her. Janiah had never spoken to him about fear, and now he said nothing. But he knew.

Then his narrative continued. "Usually there are witnesses at the challenge."

"I doubt it in this case," Janiah said.

Divine Mathematics nodded in agreement. "But one of the points in engaging in a duel is having the results known. Your prowess celebrated."

"You mean winning isn't enough?"

He smiled at her. "Winning in a situation like this is everything. It means you live. But no, it ain't enough."

Janiah looked at him quizzically.

"Go Gao needs other folks to know about his deeds. It's why he leaves the 1488 signature at the scene. It's why he takes the risks he does."

Janiah nodded. "I talked with my brother about this. He says that the killer wants to be caught."

Divine Mathematics' eyes narrowed. "He does not want to be caught, Mack. He wants to win; to humiliate me and to take revenge for my rejection. In doing so, he wants to be acknowledged. Everything else is secondary."

Off in the house, the phone rang. Tony was inside

and he picked it up. Janiah could hear the murmur of conversation as a distant background to Divine Mathematics' lecture.

"We need to remember this about Go Gao: he has a... need to kill his opponent. But the duel also feeds his spirit, his ego. He's gonna attempt to catch his opponent off guard for the duel, but he's also gonna need to follow the ritual and force the victim to acknowledge his dominance."

Janiah noticed how Divine Mathematics always spoke of the challenge like it was something that would happen to someone else, and not to him. It was an interesting way to maintain a certain objectivity.

"This need is a dangerous thing," he continued. "It makes Go Gao real focused. Driven. His opponent needs to be focused on the surroundings and ready for him at any moment. But his need for the ritual can also permit the opponent to avert disaster. Remember, this man needs to defeat his opponent, to humiliate as well as to kill. The desire will create a gap in his concentration. That's where a wise man or woman can find an opportunity for victory. And survival."

Janiah was digesting her teacher's words when her brother came outside. He seemed eager but not particularly happy.

"I got a call," he said. "We got a lead on a lone 'deep-tanned' Asian man who entered Atlanta by Greyhound a day before the Mejia murder. No record of him leaving the city. He was using a different name, but the description fits. We're canvassing the hotels now. I gotta go."

Janiah walked to the door with him. Bobo's man watched them without saying a word, tracking them across the length of the dimly lit school.

"Listen, let's give this some time to play out," Tony whispered at the door. "Stay put. There are two plainclothes dudes in a car out front, so you should be fine. I'll be back. Don't go anywhere without me." He knelt down and fiddled with his pants cuff. When he stood up, there was a compact pistol in his hand.

"Take this," he said.

"Nah, I'm good," Janiah said, waving her hands in protest.

"Take it," Tony ordered. It's my old piece. The one I used to carry before James gave me 'Big Betty'. If this dude surprises you, don't stop pulling the trigger until it's out of bullets."

"Come on, Tony," Janiah said. The little gun was heavy in her hand. "What am Janiah gonna do with this?"

"With luck, nothing," he said. "Stay put. Keep your head down and I'll be back soon."

He was out the door and Janiah was left there, peering up and down the street—ever alert for *Go Gao*—and feeling the heftiness of the *Sig Sauer P320* tug at her tired shoulder muscles.

Divine Mathematics slid up behind her in that fluid, silent way he has. He looked at the gun. "Your brother means well but he is out of his element here."

"Yes, he does," Janiah said. "And yes, he is."

They turned back inside and shut the door. The lights of the living area one floor up threw a soft glow down the stairs. Divine Mathematics and Janiah followed the light, climbing up the steps, moving soundlessly toward the brightness.

Divine Mathematics opened a drawer beneath them and removed a karambit—a small curved knife resembling a claw. The blue steel handle had a hole in it for the wielder's index finger. He slipped it into a blue leather sheath.

"Take this, too. You're better with blades."

Janiah felt a stab of panic. "What do I need any of this for?" she asked.

Janiah thought she caught a flash of impatience surge across Divine Mathematics' face. "Mack... this man does the unexpected," her teacher said. "What if he comes now and Bobo and his man aren't enough? What if he comes later and your brother fails you?" He paused. "What if you're surprised by Go Gao and he gets close?" He began pointing out the various points where major arteries would be accessible.

"Hit him here—" He touched her neck. "Here—" He moved down her leg to mimic severing the femoral artery.

"Pop him if you can," Divine Mathematics said. "But if Go Gao comes in close to attack, don't hesitate to gut him like a mullet fish."

Her phone rang. Divine Mathematics nodded toward it on the couch.

She answered the call. It was Nemesio Pena. A lot had happened since they first met, and even though Pena's name had resurfaced with Tony, Janiah had not really thought much about him lately. He was all charm on the phone, however, as if they were old friends.

"Hey, Chef Mack," he said cheerily. "How are you?"

"What's going on, Nemesio?" Janiah asked.

"Hey, I was wondering whether you could come by," he replied. "You and Divine Mathematics." A note of tension crept into his voice. Pena continued the conversation, oblivious to the silence on Janiah's end. "Something's turned up. I think you should see it."

"Oh yeah?" Janiah finally grunted.

"Yeah. Absolutely."

"Can't you tell me over the phone, Nemesio?"

"Oh. Uh… it's a little complicated," he said. "Better to come here and see what I've got." He paused, then asked, as if the thought had just sprung up, "Hey, is your brother still working on the case?"

"Yeah," she replied. "He's out chasing some lead right now."

"Well, let's hope it works out." Pena did not sound very sincere, but what else was new? "So, what do you think? Can you two come down?"

Janiah did not really want to see Pena. She had bigger concerns. She was feeling guilty about having kept Tony in the dark for so long. *Maybe the visit will help him*, she thought. She ran through the pro's and con's of Nemesio's request:

Nemesio said he had some clues that could help me. Pro.

Nemesio is a creep and it could just turn out to be a wild goose chase or some scheme for him to make money. Con.

Go Gao would come at a later hour. It's his way. There would be plenty of time to get back. We probably wouldn't miss anything if we went. Pro.

Tony told me to stay put. Con.

But this might help him out. Pro.

Janiah stopped at that point, happy with the persuasiveness of the last idea.

***

She quietly told Divine Mathematics about the call. He nodded silently in agreement. Then he stared meaningfully at the pistol still in her hand. Janiah slipped the gun into her black leather clutch bag, and tucked the sheathed karambit into her waistband.

"Where is your car?" he asked softly, to keep Bobo unaware.

"On the side of the building," she replied.

Divine Mathematics digested this, then said quietly, "You go first. I'll meet you at the car."

As Janiah moved toward the front door, Bobo's employee tried to stop her and Janiah told him she was just heading out to pick something up at the nearby *Walgreens*. The fact that he did not see Tony's gun seemed to reassure him. With a shrug, he let her go.

Janiah was glad to get out. Getting away from the tense atmosphere, from Divine Mathematics' relentless training and from the barely controlled tension of Bobo and his assassin, made the whole situation seem so unreal. Moving around the building toward her car that night, things almost felt like normal. Janiah saw the plainclothes unit sitting in the parking lot and they saw her, but nobody stopped her. They were there to watch people coming in, not going out.

Divine Mathematics appeared out of the shadows and joined her. "How'd you get out?" she asked.

"The trick to not being discovered until it's too late is to become part of the surroundings. Stealth is the art of blending in with the background, not sneaking through dark shadows," he replied.

"So you slipped out the back door while no one was looking," Janiah said with a smirk.

Divine Mathematics nodded. "Yep."

The night was hot, traffic was light, and, Atlanta had that orange glow it gets in the summer, a pulsing aura generated by the play of pollution, trapped heat, and escaping light.

Midtown at night is never really at rest. It is abuzz with late night diners and bar-hoppers and the streets are lit by the bright wash of light leaking from stores, bars and restaurants. But when Janiah slowed to get a look at the building where they were heading, the Martial Masters museum looked dark. It made her worry, and rekindled the runaway paranoia that she had recently developed.

She parked up the block and then she and Divine Mathematics walked slowly down the sidewalk toward the entrance, scanning the street for anything out of the ordinary. There was the usual traffic—sports cars with tinted windows sped by, the pulsing bass of high-end stereos clearly audible even at a distance. Pedestrians hustled past, anxious to get out of the hot night air and into some air conditioning.

When Janiah looked through the glass entrance of the museum, the lobby lights of Martial Masters were turned way down. No security guard was in sight. But when she tugged at the doors to the lobby, they opened.

"Hello?" Janiah called.

Divine Mathematics slipped in beside her and stood stock-still.

Janiah checked the doors to the office complex to her right. They were locked, which was odd—Janiah expected to find Pena there. A brief spurt of annoyance washed through her: *Is Nemesio playing games?* She wondered. But Divine Mathematics had trained her well over the years. Her body did the things it was supposed to do, even when the mind was not functioning well.

Even as a jumble of thoughts and emotions swirled within her, there was a part of her that was working systematically. It was listening; sensing; feeling.

All sorts of noises can usually be heard in places like the museum. The wash of the ventilation system, street sounds bleeding in from the outside, the muffled din of people in other parts of the building. But in the lobby of Martial Masters, the waterfall's rumble tended to mask most other sounds. Janiah could feel the faint press of cool air on her skin, the slight give of the lobby carpet under her feet. Her eyes adjusted to the dimness from the low lighting. She stood there, waiting.

And then she knew. It was a jolting rush of intuition, arriving with such clarity that Janiah found it simultaneously startling and impossible to doubt. She felt the hair on her forearms stand up, and a cold chill creep up her spine and across her shoulders.

Janiah sensed him. Was it a sound? A smell? A phantom pulse in air pressure? Divine Mathematics would say it didn't matter. It was enough that Janiah knew.

A glance at her teacher confirmed her intuition. He was immobile, but you an almost unbearable intensity built in him. He sensed danger as well.

Janiah slowed her breathing and strained in the silence for a clue. Without thinking, she crouched down slightly, knees bent, body ready to move.

On the other side of the lobby, a faint glow from the gallery and dojo area registered in her peripheral vision. Lights were on in there somewhere. Janiah and Divine Mathematics headed toward the dojo slowly, sauntering across the lobby space in front of the waterfall. Janiah could sense the minute increase of humidity the falling water created there, and she hoped that it would mask the sound of her approach, but she was also fearful that it was doing the same for Go Gao.

Because Go Gao was there, somewhere waiting.

It's not supposed to be like this, she thought. There was no backup from Tony. No trap for Divine Mathematics to spring on Go Gao. Despite her teacher's presence, Janiah felt alone, and the realization came with sickening clarity that Tony had been right all along: evil arrives on its own terms, not on ours.

Janiah imitated Divine Mathematics, creeping through the lobby. She felt like she was being pulled toward something horrible by an irresistible force. Janiah fought against it, even though she knew that she had to go in there.

Janiah was afraid. She was angry. An urge to run overcame her.

She accepted her fate. You're meant to meet him, she

thought. *Divine Mathematics trained you for this. Go Gao is in there. He's waiting for you. Janiah's thoughts calmed her and she didn't run. But she was still afraid.*

She kept moving, however. It was all she could do to maintain breathing discipline and not let the sweat that was pouring down her forehead unnerve her. Janiah blinked the salty sweat out of the corners of her eyes and moved forward, wading through an invisible force that shoved her forward and yanked me back at the same time.

Janiah whispered the Jagunjagun Oriki—the Warrior's Prayer—taught to her by Divine Mathematics years ago. She looked over at her teacher and he was whispering it, too:

"There is no deity that can excel Ogun,

Master of the battlefield,

Terror of war.

Whoever dares the elephant dares death.

Whoever dares the buffalo dares annihilation.

Whoever dares the machete-wielding Masquerade,

Desires a free invitation to go to heaven.

Ase! Ase! Ase O!"

They went in.

CHAPTER EIGHTEEN

The place had really changed since the night Janiah was last there. As things had turned out, Janiah never got to walk through the display, but the exhibits were still there, dimly shrouded in the weak security lighting. One of the major elements in the display, a facade of wood beams and shingles simulating the entrance to the Shaolin temple, jutted into the display space along one wall. A wooden gate stood symbolically across the opening. A workman's scaffolding was pushed up against the faux temple, in preparation for the dismantling of the exhibit. The performance space was still there. A few lights, recessed into the ceiling, cast sporadic circles of brightness on the floor. The rest was dense shadow.

Janiah edged into the room with Divine Mathematics, hoping her vision would adjust in time to catch Go Gao charging her. But there was no rushing attack as they entered, no figure exploding from the shadows. Instead, in the corner of her right eye was a figure that was perfectly still, as if frozen into place.

She turned to look at the figure—it was Nemesio Pena.

They moved toward Pena and the motion seemed to enliven him. He approached them and broke into a horsey grin.

"Hey, Mack," he said. "I'm glad you could come." He looked at Divine Mathematics and bowed his head in deference. "Both of you."

Divine Mathematics seemed not to hear him. He was gazing off into the room's dark corners, his head moving slowly to maximize his sensitivity to sight and sound.

"What's the deal, Nemesio?" Janiah asked, certain there was danger there. She could not believe Pena did not feel it.

He gestured toward the temple facade. "Something's turned up. I think you should see it."

"What?" she asked, raising an eyebrow.

He made a come-along motion, "You've got to see it," he said. "I can't believe it. I mean, that it would turn up." He started to head toward the temple.

Janiah grabbed his arm. The contact made his head jerk and his eyes narrow slightly.

"Nope," she said. "Right here is good enough."

He yanked his arm out of Janiah's grip, then his face broke into a sly grin and he looked first at her, then at Divine Mathematics. "It's the bokken, Mack. Yasuke's training sword. It's been returned."

"Where?" It was the first thing Divine Mathematics had said to him.

Again, Pena gestured toward the temple. "I'll show

you. There's some sort of note with it, but it's in some African tongue; I think Yoruba. Maybe you can translate, sir."

Divine Mathematics began to move along with him.

"Teacher," Janiah hissed in warning.

He held out a hand to tell her to stay put. "It's cool, Mack," he said. "Stay tight."

"Stay tight" was *Black Fists and Afros*' call to awareness. Divine Mathematics was sending Janiah an instruction. And a warning.

There was a faint light within the temple display. The gate was slightly ajar. A long, cloth-wrapped shape rested inside the temple facade, only thirty feet away. Nix was babbling away about the sword's mysterious reappearance, but Divine Mathematics paid him no heed. He was focused on the object.

In the teacher's haste, he got ahead of Pena, pushing aside the heavy gate and entering the small space. He knelt to examine the object. Pena lagged behind, resting a hand on the gate. Then, too late, Janiah saw he wasn't resting his hand, he was pushing the gate.

The gate slammed closed and the vibration shook the scaffolding. Pena made a motion and Janiah heard the metallic click as a lock snapped into place. Divine Mathematics launched himself against the gate, but for once, his timing was off. He thudded against the barrier, and the scaffolding began to shift. Janiah shouted a warning. Her teacher turned and had time to raise one arm to protect himself from the collapsing pipes and boards. Then he was knocked down.

The noise—the crash and splintering of wood, the

ringing of metal pipes as they hit the floor—was still reverberating when Janiah reached the temple. Nemesio had scuttled out of the way across the room toward a dark corner. The gate was locked and Janiah peered in to see her teacher. Divine Mathematics was looking across the room. He was cut on the head and banged up, but the most critical injury was the arm he had used to try to ward off the collapse. It was bent at an odd angle. He held it gingerly.

Janiah knelt and looked at him as well as she could through the lattice of heavy wood. "It's broken," he groaned. Janiah whirled about to find Pena, but her teacher's voice restrained her.

"Mack," he whispered, "it's a trap. Stay tight."

"Yes, sir," Janiah said, working the lock. "Now come on, let's get you out of this."

Divine Mathematics closed his eyes in resignation. "It's too late for that." He looked off into the darkness and swallowed. "You gotta go there." Janiah shook the gate in protest, but she knew what he meant. She slowly stood and turned around, away from her teacher.

Pena stood on the other side of the room and spoke. "I told you they'd come," he said.

He was talking into the darkness at the far corner. Janiah sauntered toward him and he backed away.

A low hissing sound came from the shadows. "Fool!" a deep voice shouted. "He was supposed to be restrained, not injured!"

Pena flinched at the venom in the voice from the darkness.

"I told you they'd come," Pena said again. His voice shook a bit. "Now, give me the sword."

Janiah was half-listening to the conversation, but much of her attention was on sensing the present threat and anticipating Go Gao's movements. Even as she glared at Pena, she angled herself a bit so she could catch any movement out of the corner of her eye.

"You set this up Pena," Janiah said, her voice choked with the last vestige of fear and the rise of anger. Something stirred in the darkness. Janiah turned toward the far corner of the room. Pena had started to move in that direction. Janiah watched him as he got nearer to the shadows.

For a moment, she wanted to ask why. She wanted to scream at him; at the situation; at whatever lurked across the room. But there wasn't time. Things began falling away—all the useless distractions of emotion and random thought.

There was a smooth movement in the darkness and a figure began to emerge into the light. Events were accelerating, but Janiah had the sensation of acute perception and a lengthening of time. Things appeared sharper, clearer. They moved with a slow, fluid inevitability.

Nemesio thinks he's slick, Janiah thought. *But he's way out of his league. Whatever deal he thinks he cut, Go Gao is never gonna let him walk away. After the fight's over, if Go Gao survives, he's gonna finish Pena off. No witnesses.*

Janiah couldn't let that happen because once Go Gao was done with Pena, he would go after Divine Mathematics.

Pena asked for the sword again. "No," the voice

replied. "You get it when I'm finished; when the teacher and his student are dead."

Pena was closer to him and must have caught a glimpse of the expression on Go Gao's face, because Pena stopped dead in his tracks and backed up. All the way to the door. Janiah moved into the center of the room, facing the figure, trying to remain aware of everything around her. But the background sensations were getting fainter and fainter in the face of the energy Go Gao emanated.

Janiah stood there, eyes narrowed as if they could peer through the shadow, breath rising and falling in an easy, soundless rhythm.

The figure stepped forward. He was clad in a red, short sleeve rash guard, red joggers and red suede wrestling shoes. "I'm Go Gao," he said, holding his right fist chest high and covering it with his left hand in the traditional 'Fist-Palm' salute.

Go Gao had strong Asian features. His nose was small and his cheekbones were high. He was a bit above-average height, with a running back's build. He gave the impression of having tremendous energy built by years of relentless training. His skin was medium-tan and his hair was black and curly, cut short and even.

A half-smile, grimly amused, played across his face. But Janiah could see that behind the smile, there was rage. This fury made him seem larger and more menacing. Janiah tingled with an awareness of how dangerous Go Gao was. She remembered Divine Mathematics' assessment of his skill, even at the beginning of his training with God-Body, all those years ago. How formidable was he now? She thought of the crime scenes she had studied. In her mind, she saw a fleeting image of Mejia, crumpled on that very floor. She saw the crime scene reports for Wulff and

Coutinho. And Janiah thought of James.

But now the time for thinking was at an end. Go Gao had saluted her, and she needed to return the courtesy. She knelt and saluted in the *Black Fists and Afros* way.

"Don't let your eyes drop from him," Divine Mathematics had told her back at the school. Janiah didn't.

She looked at him again, as if truly seeing him for the first time. On the street, you merely look at people. Here, Janiah needed to *see*. What she saw was no longer just the typical visual impression you get of a person; she observed the elements that would help her form a strategy.

Go Gao smiled and gestured to the floor. It was a very tight smile, a social nicety and not a barometer of an internal state. His white teeth glittered.

They both sat down warily, simultaneously obeying the dictates of etiquette and watching, alert for the slightest offensive movement. They were tightly coiled and ready for action.

Janiah's focus was locked on Go Gao's sternum. Her face was calm and expressionless.

Go Gao raised his voice but never took his eyes off her. "You've taught her well, Divine Mathematics."

Janiah could hear the faint rustle of movement as Divine Mathematics, in evident pain, stood and addressed the killer.

"There's no need for this," Divine Mathematics said.

"The hell there isn't," Go Gao said with venom. "There's every reason. I've dreamed of this. For years, I hurt from your rejection... I hated you for making me murder

REK." You could see the rage building within him, leaking out as he spoke.

"Go Gao!" Divine Mathematics said. "Keep my sister out of your rotten ass mouth!"

It took a visible effort for Go Gao to calm himself. "You had to be taught a lesson," he said. "A teacher must share his or her knowledge with the next generation, not keep it to himself. But you... you don't train military... you don't teach non-Black people... no matter how much potential that potential student has; no matter how much they beg you. So judgmental."

Go Gao rose slowly and walked toward Divine Mathematics, gazing at him as you would at a caged animal. There was contempt in his face. But Go Gao only moved a few steps in the old teacher's direction. Janiah sensed fear in the killer, as well.

"I knew someday that I would face you, Divine Mathematics," Go Gao said. "I've worked for years to perfect myself. To be able to show you just how wrong you were for rejecting me."

"You call me judgmental," Divine Mathematics said. "But you are a white supremacist... and you aren't even white. You self-hating fool."

Go Gao snorted in disgust. "Niggers are weak! *You're* weak. To think, all these years, I hesitated to confront you." Go Gao laughed, a hard, short noise with no joy in it. "I should have seen earlier how weak you really are. You are a nigger, after all."

"Let me out," Divine Mathematics said. "And we'll see how weak this 'nigger' is."

Go Gao's eyes glinted as he smiled. "In time. If that

idiot Pena had not damaged you, it would have been glorious. As it is now, it will merely be the end of my ritual." Go Gao glided back toward the center of the room, where Janiah stood. He continued speaking but with his back to the teacher. "Life's surprises are endless. And I have always struggled to see the purpose in it." He sighed. "You've helped me see, old man. You've brought me humiliation and hurt... now disappointment. But after all this time, I've come to really see. There's a curious liberation to it all—a sense of being untethered; free of restraint and able to act as you wish. It took me years to forge my will to this end."

His eyes didn't really seem like they were registering Janiah's presence; they were focused on some inner reality. But now they bore into her. "You wouldn't understand, woman. You mugou never grasp the essence of the art."

"Mugou?" Janiah said. "Sounds like a bad chicken stir-fry."

"Mugou means 'bitch'," Go Gao said, frowning. "Which you prove you are by your comment."

"I think I've grasped the fact that you're crazy as shit," Janiah said with a smirk.

Go Gao smiled ruefully and shook his head. "Of course. You can't see it." Again his voice was raised for Divine Mathematics' benefit. "You've made many mistakes, old man. You should have never turned me away."

"You can never win when self-pity is your armor and whining is your sword," Divine Mathematics said.

"Such a wretched nigger," Go Gao spat. Then he returned to his thoughts. "You should have never come to this country. You've squandered your heritage. Africans are givers."

"Yeah, we gave others our math and medicine and architecture and commerce and other sciences and they turned around and used them to enslave and oppress us," Divine Mathematics said.

Go Gao waved off Divine Mathematics' words then spoke to Janiah. "You think I'm a madman, woman? Because of the murders?" He chuckled. "You can't see. These acts are... ceremonies for the gods. They're pure; honest. They lay bare the heart of things. When the fight is done, you can't imagine the feeling... the sense of... fusion to the world of spirits." He smiled again. "And it's done on my terms."

Divine Mathematics shook his head and said, "This has gotta end, Go Gao."

It was a strain for Janiah to just wait there, listening to them and waiting for the ritual to unfold. Down deep, she could feel the currents swirling about the room. Despite the flow of words and the smiles, there was tension there. She could feel it building slowly, ratcheting up.

"So, to the task at hand," Go Gao said calmly as he knelt again. He sat up a bit straighter and said, "I am Go Gao—"

"Formerly of God-Body," Janiah said, interrupting him, just to rattle him a bit. Some of the true danger in Go Gao briefly shot out from his eyes, escaping from behind the barrier he had placed there.

"I am a sifu and student of Chow Gar Tong Long— Southern Praying Mantis," Go Gao continued. "My teacher is my father, Jing Sheng Gao; his teacher is Yip Shui, whose teacher is Lao Soei, whose teacher is Wong Fook Go, whose teacher is the founder of Chow Gar, the magnanimous Chow Ah Naam. I have killed four men in duels. I would like to compare."

Dang, there are more victims than we were aware of, Janiah thought.

Go Gao gave the fist-palm salute toward her at the conclusion of his recital. It was her turn.

"I am Janiah Mack," Janiah began. "I am a full instructor and student of Ijakadi and Fifty-Two Blocks. My teacher is Divine Mathematics, whose teachers are Ogunyemi Akinsegun and Supreme Justice Allah. I have killed no man in a duel."

Go Gao grinned at her.

"Until tonight," she concluded.

His grin grew wider; his eyes, colder.

He stood up suddenly, and so did Janiah, as if they were connected by a string. Go Gao was watching, and he nodded in mock approval. He gestured languidly to the side of the dojo.

"Here are weapons for you to choose from."

"Why me?" Janiah asked.

He paused and looked at her. "Why you?"

Janiah just nodded.

"You are his disciple, right?"

Janiah didn't answer and he didn't seem to care. Part of her was glad to have him talk; it gave her time to prepare.

"Your teacher rejected me. That rejection broke my

mind; destroyed my life," Go Gao said. "I've trained for years, and now I will destroy him. But before that, I will take away what he values most."

He paused and eyed her speculatively. "Have you been a teacher, Ms. Mack? Do you know what matters most to a master? It's not life that is precious—warriors are trained not to fear death." He glared at her, barely masking his fury. "Before I kill him, I want him to know that I've destroyed everything he has worked to create. I'm going to take away his most prized student, Ms. Mack. I'm going to kill you."

He gestured again. A black wrestling mat had been placed on the floor. A wooden katana, a wooden machete and two middle staffs lay at the edge of the mat. Janiah moved cautiously toward them, stepping sideways to keep Go Gao to her front.

"And you?" she asked, gesturing at the weapons.

He faded back into the shadows and emerged, holding a familiar weapon. It was the katana Janiah had seen in Pena's photos.

"You took it," Janiah said.

He drew the weapon from its scabbard. The steel hissed faintly against the case. Go Gao regarded the blade admiringly as the light winked along its length. "The opportunity was... unexpected. But a warrior must act decisively."

Then Go Gao gestured with it. "As I told Mr. Pena, I still have some use for this weapon."

He came toward her and opened his arms wide, the sword in his right hand. Janiah put down the karambit her teacher had given her then lay the pistol next to it. Then she picked up a middle staff.

He smiled. "The middle staff, Ms. Mack?" he said. "I had hoped for more of a challenge. You should have kept the pistol." He sighed and slowly sheathed the sword. "Very well. Let's play a little." He set down the sword and stooped to grasp a bokken.

"I'm surprised you didn't bring a dao," Janiah said.

"If Pena had a sword from my homeland as well-crafted as the Japanese ones, I would have taken it, instead," Go Gao said. "I would have thought you'd pick the machete."

"Figured I'd mix things up," she said with a shrug.

Really, part of her just liked the middle staff and she was skilled with it.

They stood facing each other in the ready position. The middle staff was longer than the wooden sword, but the bokken was heavier. Go Gao watched Janiah briefly, his eyes expressionless and his body relaxed. Then the attack came.

They say the thing that marks a true master is not the force behind an attack, but the speed it's launched with. When Go Gao moved, it was a blur. Janiah whipped the middle staff up to meet the strike, parrying it as she awaited the opportunity to counter.

Go Gao was so quick, however, recognizing that was impossible. Things were happening so rapidly that the moves seemed to merge into a fluid sequence, a continuum of extreme violence and all Janiah could do was parry and evade the murderer's blows. The middle staff met the bokken and directed it away from Janiah's face. Go Gao slid the wooden sword forward and in along the length of the middle staff. Janiah drew the staff back into a reverse posture, disengaging from the bokken, but the killer pressed forward. Janiah slid to her right, then whipped the staff up, around, and down toward Go Gao's head.

He skittered backward and the head-end of the staff just missed him.

They spun and surged through the alternating areas of darkness and light in the room. The effect was strobe-like. The struggle pulsed and jerked in the alternating light levels. Janiah could feel her eyes straining as she tried to follow and anticipate Go Gao's attacks.

At one point, there was a small hesitation in his back-step. Janiah leapt at the opening it presented.

The staff came whistling down from high on her right toward his collarbone.

Go Gao just managed to pull back from the strike. The tip of the weapon sped down toward the floor.

Janiah allowed the momentum to carry her past him. She then thrust the tail-end of the middle staff backward and upward under her left forearm.

The tip of the middle staff nicked his ear.

Janiah whirled backward to her right toward Go Gao then slammed a reverse elbow strike into the bloody side of his head.

Go Gao stumbled sideways. Janiah closed with the staff and struck down on his right hand. The staff landed with a *crack* at the base of his thumb. He grunted in pain.

Go Gao darted away. Janiah could tell that he could not wield the bokken well anymore—his right thumb was probably broken.

Janiah pressed him, advancing with the head of the staff pointed at his throat.

Go Gao exploded in a lateral dive. Landing among the weapons on the floor, he unsheathed the katana before Janiah could get to him.

The katana, actually lighter than its wooden replica, could be wielded with only one hand.

Lights caught on the highly polished surface of the blade. He rose from the floor in a fluid motion. Janiah sidestepped and readied herself for the new threat.

Go Gao exploded toward her. Janiah detected a slight drop of the sword's tip, which comes before a strike. It was an error, and Janiah should have been suspicious. Well-trained martial artists like Go Gao rarely make such mistakes, but she was drawn to the apparent flaw. The end of her staff touched the side of his blade. Janiah tried to follow the katana up as Go Gao pulled it over his head for the strike, but suddenly, he hopped forward with his left foot raised, and brought his heel down with a stomping kick directed at her right thigh.

It was a bone-breaking move. Janiah had to collapse her leg and fall with the direction of the kick in order to save her thigh from being shattered.

His foot still smashed into her with an almost paralyzing force.

Janiah rolled sideways, desperate to avoid the sword's blade. She stood, trying to test weight on her leg—which felt numb and wobbly—without letting him see the damage he had caused.

Janiah attacked. Her hurt leg made things awkward. The attack faltered. Go Gao shuffled backward slightly. Janiah was overcommitted and felt herself toppling toward him, losing her balance.

He shuffled backward again, trying to pull her in more.

Janiah scrambled to regain her footing, but the damage to the muscles in her leg made it sluggish and clumsy. Go Gao loomed before her, katana raised.

Instinctively, Janiah turned away, flinching from the blow about to come. She heard the temple gate crash open and a shout from Divine Mathematics. Her teacher shot across her line of vision and rammed into Go Gao. But the younger man deflected him and continued to move in on Janiah. Divine Mathematics fell hard and collapsed in a heap. She heard the whistle of the sword as it arced down. It bit into the ribs in her back.

Janiah fell. She knew that she should keep moving, but for a brief second, she was shocked into stillness. Then Go Gao was on her.

He had dropped the sword, wanting to experience the pleasure of beating Janiah to death with his bare hands. She was slumped there, half-sitting, holding herself up with an arm. Go Gao came up behind her and his muscular arm circled her neck. The other hand pushed against the back of her head, forcing her throat against the arm.

Janiah knew she had about five seconds before the pressure on her neck cut off the flow of blood to her brain. After that, the world would turn gray, then black. The only thing Janiah had going for her was the fact that one of Go Gao's hands was less than fully functional. Janiah tried to squirm into a better position, but he was up against her from behind, and the gash in her back seemed to be limiting her ability to move.

She struggled against the pressure he was exerting. The vertebrae in her neck made little popping sounds as she tried to resist the force of the choke. Go Gao spoke in her ear:

"That night after the performance, I had hoped to finish this with your master, but you interfered. He escaped, but I will take his life soon. He values you. I see this. So now, I will take you from him. It will destroy him. You're beaten, Ms. Mack. Say it." He squeezed a little tighter. "Say it." His tone almost sounded like a giggle, except the voice was too raspy, too deadly serious. "Say it and I might let him live." He paused. "Then again, maybe I won't."

Part of her was listening, but part of her was somewhere else. Divine Mathematics had told her this gap would appear. Go Gao's need for recognition. For dominance. He was playing with her, but it was important to him that she responded to him. Janiah could feel the arm slowly tighten around her neck as he talked, building to a final, mighty squeeze.

Janiah did not need to move her jaw too far. She opened her mouth as wide as she could and bit into Go Gao's arm. She tried to force her upper and lower teeth to meet as they tore through his flesh. His muscles jumped against Janiah's tongue as she worked. The hand that pressed the back of her head actually forced her mouth deeper for a split second, then the pressure was gone.

Her ears were ringing from the approach of a blackout, but his howl was clear. He released his hold on her then scrambled away, reaching for the sword again.

Janiah leapt toward him.

Go Gao was on his knees, reaching for the blade, when Janiah slammed into him from behind. He flew forward, and with the force of the impact, his head actually whiplashed, smacking into Janiah's face. She heard the bone in her nose *crack*.

Janiah grabbed Go Gao's right arm with both of hers then forced his arm behind his back in a chicken-wing lock. He lay there for a second, face down, squirming, but fighting the joint lock caused too much pain. The killer stopped squirming.

Janiah could feel the strain the lock was putting on the joint of his right shoulder. Go Gao grunted and turned his head toward her. The side of his face and head was bloody. Janiah could see his right eye roll back into the corner to stare at her. The glare was steady and dark and malevolent.

Then he began, very slowly and systematically, to force the shoulder dislocation that would let him escape the joint-lock. And all the while, he stared at Janiah.

Janiah yanked Go Gao's arm straight and out to the side then slammed the bone of her forearm on his triceps tendon, just behind his elbow as she pulled his wrist upward. His elbow made a sickening *pop*, then Go Gao yelped in agony.

Janiah slammed her elbow into the killer's neck, just below his ear. She grunted from the tearing sensation the attack made in her back. She fought back the pain and slammed another elbow, then did it again... and again... and again.

Go Gao's convulsed violently then went limp.

CHAPTER NINETEEN

Janiah slumped back on the floor, spitting out the taste of Go Gao's blood. She felt sick.

She dragged herself away from the Go Gao's still form.

The wooden floor was a slick, bloody mess. She stood up, but a wave of nausea hit her and she vomited onto the bloody mat. She slumped against a wall.

Divine Mathematics approached. He was carrying the cloth bundle that held Yasuke's sword. He looked her over and said. "We gotta go. Quickly." But before they left, he walked over to Go Gao's body. He stared at the killer for a moment, then stooped and picked up the katana.

They shuffled out into the lobby. Pena was waiting there.

"Ms. Mack," he said, looking her up and down, taking in the damage. Then he spotted the swords in Divine Mathematics' hand.

"Hey, great," he said brightly. "Thanks, I'll take those."

Divine Mathematics stared, stone-faced.

"No," Janiah told him.

"What do you mean, 'no'?" Pena said with a frown.

"They'll look good in the school," Divine Mathematics said.

Pena seemed not to hear.

"It was the insurance, wasn't it?" Janiah asked. Her nose was still bleeding.

"I need those back," Pena said. "They're supposed to be covered for a hundred fifty g's each," he said. "Give them to me."

"I think we'll hold on to them," Janiah said.

"They're mine," Pena said in protest. He moved like he was going to keep Janiah and Divine Mathematics from leaving the lobby. Janiah saw he had her karambit in his hands.

Janiah took a deep breath. It made a ragged sound. "Pena, get your ass out of the way or I'll take that knife away and gut you."

Pena backed down. He dropped the knife. It clattered to the floor, and they inched their way out. Janiah heard a series of faint beeps beneath the din of the rushing waterfall. Janiah turned to look at Pena. He was holding a cell phone in his hand.

"We'd better move," she said to Divine Mathematics.

But they were already there.

Pena must have had these two goons standing by

outside the building, Janiah thought.

The goons popped out of a parked sedan and stood on the sidewalk. They were both big, with thick upper torsos and waists that looked smaller than a thirteen-year old ballerina's. One of them had a brushed back, hot-combed, salt-and-pepper afro that made him look like a cross between Frederick Douglass and Al Sharpton. He seemed to be in charge. The lapels of his black, open-collared shirt were neatly spread out over his black sports coat. Beads in alternating red and black colors hung around his neck and on his chest. He was fawn-brown and had little wrinkles at the corners of his eyes. He regarded Janiah and Divine Mathematics calmly.

His younger partner's ruddy head was shaved and he had a closely trimmed goatee. He wore a black sports coat as well, but the shirt underneath it was a black t-shirt. A pair of shades dangled from his jacket pocket. He turned his head from one direction to the other, checking out the surroundings, or looking for witnesses.

"C'mon, man, let's go," the younger man said.

His partner did not respond and continued to peer closely at Janiah.

"Good googly moogly," the salt-and-pepper-haired man said. "What happened to y'all?"

"Bad night," Janiah answered.

"No shit," the older goon said. His eyes shifted to a spot behind her.

It's probably Pena coming out to join the party, Janiah thought.

"Well, no need for more trouble," the older goon went

on. "Go ahead and give me Mr. Pena's swords, and we can all call it a night." He sounded very reasonable.

"Nah," Janiah said.

The older goon looked at her with disappointment.

The young one started to move toward Janiah and Divine Mathematics. As he did, he reached into his jacket and pulled out a Glock 31—.357 pistol.

"Man, this is bullshit," the young goon said. "Let's do this chick and the old man, grab the stuff, and get the fuck outta here."

As the young man was moving toward them, Janiah could see over his shoulder. The headlights of a car were getting bigger fast. The car swerved a little as it sped up the street. Someone was in a hurry. The sound of the revving car engine made the young man turn around.

The vehicle bounced up the curb, clipping a fire hydrant, and jerked to a stop on the sidewalk. The driver's door flew open before the car stopped, rocking on its springs.

"Don't move!" the driver screamed. It was hard to see in the dark, but the shape of a gun pointing through the space between the open door of the car and the windshield came into view.

The young goon started to turn toward the voice.

"I said don't move!" the driver shouted.

The young goon's gun came up.

"Cody," the older one called out. But it was too late.

Janiah dove out of the way. Divine Mathematics was

right behind her. The young thug fired. The muzzle flash briefly highlighted his silhouette. Then three shots rang out from the car, and three holes opened in the young man's chest, driving him backward. He crumpled onto the sidewalk.

The older thug stood with his hands in the air, not moving a muscle.

Tony came out from behind the passenger side of the car. "Janiah?"

Janiah felt dizzy and sat down on the pavement by the curb. She hoped it was cooler there. She hoped there would be more air. She held her head in her hands and closed her eyes. Blood roared in her ears as she gulped for air. She listened to the sounds around her.

Tony's voice got closer. Janiah heard Cody's gun skitter across the cement as Tony kicked it away. Then she heard the click of handcuffs.

"Thank God, you're here." Pena's voice was filled with fake relief.

"Shut the fuck up, Pena," Tony told him. Sirens howled in the distance.

Janiah opened her eyes as a new set of lights appeared on the scene. They were from Bobo's black Lexus. The illumination glittered across a dark pool that slowly spread from Cody's body and oozed into the street. Janiah sniffed and a drop of blood spattered, fat and round, down between her feet.

Then another cop car pulled up, lights cycling around, and two uniformed police jumped out.

"Janiah, you okay?" Tony shouted at her.

Janiah didn't answer.

"Divine Mathematics," Tony said, turning to Janiah's teacher. "Is she okay?"

Janiah felt Divine Mathematics' hands on her, keeping her upright.

"She'll be fine after some rest," Divine Mathematics replied.

Janiah nodded in affirmation. It hurt to do it.

Then Tony sauntered over to the handcuffed goon with the Frederick Douglass-Al Sharpton hair.

"Well, if it isn't Scorpio," Tony said. "What brings you here?"

"Just passing by, Mack," Scorpio replied. "No news story for you here."

"Who's the dead dude?"

Scorpio shrugged. It was the first time he had moved since his accomplice had been shot. "Hell if I know," he said. "Some unlucky white dude." He looked at Tony, who nodded in return.

"Sure," Tony said.

Bobo slid out of his car, spotted Janiah swooning at the curb with Divine Mathematics beside her, and strode over. His assassin was with him, vigilant and confused at the same time.

"Divine Mathematics, where is he?"

"Hey, I'm bleeding," Janiah said, interrupting him.

"No shit, Sherlock," Tony said as he came up to the other side of her. With Divine Mathematics' help, he helped her lie down.

"I need to know where he is," Bobo insisted. He sounded like he was going to explode.

Tony ignored him and knelt down beside Janiah. "How you doin', sis?"

"How'd you know where I was?" Janiah asked, her voice weak.

"Divine Mathematics called before he left."

Janiah tried to smile, but it hurt her nose. She swiveled her head around to look at Divine Mathematics. He smiled. Then Janiah squinted at Bobo "He's in there," Janiah told him.

Bobo and the assassin disappeared into the building.

The EMTs arrived on the scene. They turned Janiah on her side while they cut the back of her top open and prepped her. "You a good guy or bad guy... err, girl... err, woman?" one asked. It didn't slow his actions down any; he was just making small talk.

"Huh?" Janiah said.

The EMT looked at Tony. Tony pointed to the dead goon. "Bad," he said. Then he pointed at Janiah. "Good." He looked at Divine Mathematics for a minute, then pointed at him. "Good-ish."

Divine Mathematics laughed.

The EMT nodded.

They loaded Janiah up into the ambulance while

another team checked out Divine Mathematics. Before the ambulance doors closed, she saw Bobo and his assassin emerge from the building. They slipped into their car and drove off. No need to attract attention.

Tony stood at the doors of the ambulance. "These guys will take care of you," he told Janiah. "Divine Mathematics is in another unit. I'll follow y'all."

Janiah gave him a little grin and tried to wink. "Hold onto our swords," she said.

The doors closed and they strapped her in. Then they put the oxygen mask on her and she tried to relax as they hit every pothole in Midtown Atlanta on the way to the hospital.

CHAPTER TWENTY

The summer months were almost at an end, but the heat lingered. Janiah could still feel it through her blue blazer even though she sat in an air-conditioned room. The melding of heat and coolness felt good. Her back wound had healed, but her muscles were still tight where the sword had sliced through them, and Janiah found herself drowsing, lulled by the speech she was listening to that went on and on.

Janiah was attending Divine Mathematics' induction into the Hall of Fame of the *World Grandmasters' Council.*

Nearly five thousand martial arts masters, instructors, students and family members of inductees were in attendance. Everyone was dressed in well-tailored suits or the traditional ceremonial wear of their cultures.

The press from all over America and other countries was present, and the cameras were rolling. Tony went back and forth between reporting the news and sitting with Janiah in the second row. They were on the end, far enough away to be able to make fun of things.

Tony screwed his mouth around to the side. "I bet I

could take half of these masters."

Janiah smiled and leaned her head toward him. "The ones in their nineties, maybe."

In front of them, Divine Mathematics sat shaking his head at their conversation without looking back at them.

"I got popcorn," James said, sliding gingerly into the seat next to Tony. "Man, that line was long." He was thin and moved stiffly and with caution.

Go Gao was dead. Janiah learned that from the police who came to get her statement at the hospital. Through the buzz of weariness and painkillers, she gave them her version of things. Tony later told her that Go Gao had been found face up, a *karambit* rammed deep into his chest.

"You had already broken Go Gao's neck, Janiah, but you had to stab him after he was dead, too?" he had said. "You're colder than a polar bear's toenails."

They both knew that Janiah had not used the knife. No one really paid much attention when Bobo and his assassin slipped into Martial Masters. Janiah thought back to glimpsing them emerging a few minutes later, hustling away into the night. They were pretty sure Bobo had used the knife. The police later discouraged any close inquiries about it. When Tony pressed things, the executives at Fox told him to drop it or else.

Divine Mathematics later told her that he always knew Go Gao would come one day and would try to kill her first. He waited until she was out of the hospital to share that.

"You knew all that time that he would come for me?" she had asked. "And you didn't say anything?" Janiah was shocked and hurt.

Divine Mathematics gazed at her. He was calm and totally sure of himself. "Of course I didn't," he said. "Think of what it would have done to your training; your life, period. It was a distraction you didn't need."

"But what if he had killed me, Teacher?" Janiah said in exasperation.

"If 'ifs' and 'buts' were candies and nuts, every day would be Christmas."

Later, after watching her brood, Divine Mathematics took up the issue again. "Mack, I've train for years and, with time, I began to see that there was potential." He took a breath and paused briefly. "The selection of a Chief Instructor ain't easy and a lot of times, it's marked by blood."

Janiah was angry for a time, but she knew that, as a master, Divine Mathematics pushes you to do things you never would have dared do yourself and at the end, you're not exactly grateful, but you *are* changed for the better.

Janiah heard that a friend of Tony's was writing a book about the murders. The book would be filled with all the case's dark overtones and twisted logic—theories of abuse, feelings of rejection and the need for recognition. The urge to break free and yet to belong, to seek out authority figures, to become like them. To destroy them. The need to get close to what we can't have but crave desperately. Janiah could follow the argument on an intellectual level, she supposed, but she had little interest left in the case. She wanted to only light in her life.

A polite rippling of applause made Janiah sit up a bit straighter and open her eyes.

The long ritual of receiving awards, congratulating recipients and shameless self-promotion eventually petered out into a champagne reception.

Divine Mathematics stood to one side staring at the crowd and bobbing his head to the song *Ordinary People*, by John Legend.

Janiah, Tony and James stood by the bar for a while. James leaned on it. They can do amazing things with microsurgery, but Janiah still couldn't believe that they reattached his hand. Even in the afternoon sun, Janiah got a chill. For a moment, she could smell the dampness and blood on the subway platform.

Janiah nodded at Tony's reattached hand. "How's the therapy going?"

He gingerly rotated his hand and moved each finger with effort, as if a weight was attached to each one. Then he grinned up at Janiah. "It's going slow and hurts like a mug, but it's better than having a doggone hook."

Janiah was identifying the well known masters and MMA champions at the reception to Tony and James when Divine Mathematics walked up and introduced the lawyer, Kachina White-Eagle, to them.

"Ms. Mack," she said as she unzipped his little folder, "I'm pleased to be able to present you with the reward for the return of Yasuke's sword." Her voice was elegant, rich and precise. "Here is a check for forty-thousand dollars, as discussed."

Janiah nodded, and fished a piece of paper out of her pocket. "Ms. White-Eagle," I'm honored, but I'd be grateful if you'd have separate checks made out in three names."

Ms. White-Eagle took the paper Janiah gave her and

frowned. Divine Mathematics murmured something and the lawyer's expression cleared. Then she placed her folder down on one of the cocktail tables and carefully filled out blank checks with the names. Ms. White-Eagle finished writing, made some notes on a form, and asked Janiah to sign to acknowledge receipt of the reward. Janiah did.

Ms. White-Eagle zipped up her folder, nodded and then left.

Janiah stared at the checks Kachina White-Eagle had given to her. Then, with a grin, she handed one to Tony and one to James. "Don't spend it all on booze," Janiah said.

The two men looked at her. For once, her brother seemed at a loss for words. He nodded and said, "Thanks, Janiah."

Divine Mathematics smiled at her. "You're a good student, Mack."

From him, that was saying a lot. Janiah kissed him on his cheek. "I'm a slow learner, Teacher." Sometimes she still dreamed about the fight with Go Gao, and the scars on her back still burned.

Divine Mathematics' squinted. "Naw," he said to her. "Any fool can throw a punch or stab somebody. You've got good character, too." He took a final sip of champagne. "Thank y'all, for coming out." The old master set his glass down, nodded to them all, and turned to go. He flowed through the crowd and out of sight.

After a while, Janiah quietly wandered into the courtyard behind the headquarters building of the *World Grandmasters' Council.*

It was quieter out there and smelled of watermelon

and honeysuckle. It seemed like an okay place to be.

Tony came up to her. "What now?"

Janiah shrugged. "Your guess is as good as mine."

"What do you think," he said, "You got time for one more drink?"

They looked at the crowd that was starting to fill the courtyard, eyed each other, and smiled, then spoke simultaneously: "Nah."

"I gotta go," Tony said. "Barbecue tomorrow?"

"Fo' sho'."

Tony patted her shoulder. He started to say something, but stopped.

They nodded at each other—a recognition of things shared that are beyond words. Tony went back for James.

Janiah stood for a while, enjoying the sensation of just being alive. Then she walked off. *I gotta go to bed early*, she thought. *Class is in the morning.*

ABOUT THE AUTHOR

As a former combat veteran (MOS: 18F), Master and Technical Director of the Afrikan Martial Arts Institute and Co-Chair of the Urban Survival and Preparedness Institute, Balogun Ojetade is the author of the bestselling non-fiction books *Afrikan Martial Arts: Discovering the Warrior Within*, *The Afrikan Warriors Bible*, *Surviving the Urban Apocalypse*, *The Urban Self Defense Manual*, *The Young Afrikan Warriors' Guide to Defeating Bullies & Trolls*, *Never Unarmed: The Afrikan Warriors' Guide to Improvised Weapons*, *Ofo Ase: 365 Daily Affirmations to Awaken the Afrikan Warrior Within*, *Ori: The Afrikan Warriors' Mindset*, *Ogun Ye! Protecting the Afrikan Family and Community*, *Kori O: Protecting Afrikan Children from Violence & Sexual Abuse*, and *SKG: The Black Man & Woman's Guide to Sticks, Knives and Guns*.

He is one of the leading authorities on Afrofuturism and Afroretroism—film, fashion or fiction that combines African and/or African American culture with a blend of "retro" styles and futuristic technology, in order to explore the themes of tension between past and future and between the alienating and empowering effects of technology and on Creative Resistance. He writes about Afrofuturism/Afroretroism—Sword & Soul, Rococoa, Steamfunk and Dieselfunk at http://chroniclesofharriet.com/.

He is author of twenty-five novels and gamebooks – *MOSES: The Chronicles of Harriet Tubman (Books 1 & 2)*; *The Chronicles of Harriet Tubman: Freedonia*; *Redeemer*; *Once Upon A Time In Afrika*; *Fist of Africa*; *A Single Link*; *Wrath of the Siafu*; *The Scythe*; *The Keys*; *Redeemer: The Cross Chronicles*; *Beneath the Shining Jewel*; *Q-T-Pies: The Savannah Swan Files (Book 0)* and *A Haunting in the*

SWATS: The Savannah Swan Files (Book 1); *Siafu Saves the World*; *Siafu vs. The Horde*; *Dembo's Ditty*; *The Beatdown*; *Initiate 16*; *Gunsmoke Blues*; *Malik: Confessions of a Black Identity Extremist*; *Malik: Confessions of a Black Identity Extremist 2: Enemy of the State*; *Granma's Hand*; *Kill City* and *Steamfunkateers: The Steamfunk Role Playing Game* and the Steamfunkateers adventure, *The Haunting of the House of Crum*—contributing co-editor of three anthologies: *Ki: Khanga: The Anthology*, *Steamfunk* and *Dieselfunk* and contributing editor of the *Rococoa* anthology and *Black Power: The Superhero Anthology*.

He is also the creator and author of the Afrofuturistic manga series, *Jagunjagun Lewa (Pretty Warrior)* and author/co-creator of the *Ice Cold Carter* photo-graphic novel series.

Finally, he is co-author of the award winning screenplay, *Ngolo* and co-creator of *Ki Khanga: The Sword and Soul Role-Playing Game*, both with author Milton Davis.

Reach him on Facebook at https://www.facebook.com/Afrikan.Martial.Arts and on Instagram at @balogun_ojetade and @afrikanmartialarts. Find his books on *Amazon* at https://www.amazon.com/Balogun-Ojetade/e/B00AVEA7SU.

Made in the USA
Columbia, SC
01 September 2019